THE FAMILY

A PHILADELPHIA MOB STORY

ANTONNE M. JONES

ELDON PUBLISHING COMPANY
PHILADELPHIA, PENNSYLVANIA
P.O. Box 54742
www.eldon-pub.com

EXCERPT FROM "GRAND PUBA" appears on the song
"Wake up" by Brand Nubian
EXCERPT FROM "CHUCK D" Appears on the song
"Welcome to The Terror Dome" by Public Enemy
EXCERPT FROM "SADAT X Appear on the song
"'Concerto in the X Minor" by Brand Nubian
EXCERPT FROM "KRS.1" Appears on the "Live and
Hardcore" by KRS 1
EXCERPT FROM "U GOD" Appears on the Ironman
Album by Ghostface Killah
EXCERPT FROM "RAKIM" Appears on the song "Teach
the Children" by Eric Band Rakim
EXCERPT FROM "NAS" Appears on Funkmaster Flex
volume ll.
COVER PHOTOGRAPH BY: MOFFA STUDIO
POSED BY: ANTONNE M. JONES
AND RONALD WELTON, JR.
COVER DESIGN BY: SAT ONE.
Stylist Gene: Philadelphia Hair Co.

Dazzling!! Oprah will love this book, as well as the author.

Better than "New Jack City", more intriguing that "Scarface", and the electricity of "Goodfellas". Van Peeple's, De Palma's, and Scorcese's dream script.

Entertains from cover to cover. A reality check for "wanna be" criminals.

Finally, a book with modern day language of urban Americans. This will mark the beginning of dispelling the stereotype stating that "Black men do not read". Unbelievable!!

A book belonging in prisons, libraries, law schools, and the archives.

In Loving Memory

Lionel Rhodan
Kareem Fischer
Sterling Cornell
John Preston
Aquil Shaheed Ford
John Riddick
Timothy Kitt
Charles "Chuckie" Jones
Tiffany Westbrook
Nicole Potter
Kevin Hawkins
Buckie
And
Little Man

A Message from the Author
(Potent Quotables)

... A drug controlled substance contained
in a vial, sent it by the devil as he looks
then he smiles
>   - Grand Puba

It is weak to speak and blame
somebody else when you
destroy yourself...
>   - Chuck D

... I wanted to get violent but I
am a lover of black mothers
and black mothers need sons'
not children who have been
killed by guns.
>   - Sadat X

If negativity comes with a "22",
positivity comes with a "45"
>   - KRS.1

Some people don't have no
direction because they don't
know the signs of their
self, Everything that is in the
universe, that has created the
universe, exists within you.

                              - U. God

Keep on building,
because we got to keep building
till the answers are filled in
and make sure you don't stop until
then and if you do, remember the
children.

                              - Rakim

God painted me black,
thanks for that.

                              - Nas Escobar

This book is dedicated to my family and all of the friends who have supported my thoughts and gave me the strength to carry them out. Also, to my beautiful mother who put up with all of my big dream stories but had never hesitated to remind me to always have something to fall back on. I did have something; you, and I love you for that. This book is also dedicated to the dead and incarcerated brothers and sisters who fell into the devil's trap. And for those who fight for the cause, keep fighting until we get what we want as well as what we deserve. Once we cross that bridge then they will know that it is on!

The Family

During the process of me ruining my own black people, by making crack readily available to them, like most fruitless drug dealers in the hood, I had always attempted to fault the white man for my own misconduct.

But the white man did not conspire with me to purchase the automatic weapons that paralyzed the little boy who was caught in the middle of crossfire resulting from a drug war.

He also did not have anything to do with me filling up the plastic vials with a substance that destroyed my neighbors' beautiful daughter which made her a prostitute to support her addiction for crack and my addiction to get a pair of Gucci's.

Towards the end of my fallen celebrity status, where were these so-called friends that I had referred to as part of my posse when I needed a character witness? Not one of these motherfuckers showed up during the trial to testify on my behalf. "The black John Gotti."

How could that be when he received life and I got death? Maybe justice ain't color-blind.

2

The Family

CHAPTER 1

To Lauryn,

Hey baby! How have you and the children been doing? I just started writing this letter because you and the kids have been on my mind all day. Earlier in the day, I had cafeteria duty in the chow hall. When I was finished cleaning up, I was mad tired, so I took a nap for a couple hours before I started writing. Boo, I want to apologize to you for all of the wrong and hurtful things I have done to you in the past. Now I realize that you have always been the only person to stand by my side through the thick and the thin, but for some inexplicable reason it seems as though I have treated you the worst. Baby, I wish that I could turn the hands of time back. But I can't. If I could I would do so many things different. For starters, I would have never chosen the kind of lifestyle that I have lived. Choosing that kind of life was the biggest mistake that I have ever made. Lauryn, I cry almost every night since I've been in here because this was not the way that I had our lives planned. I can now clearly see that my promiscuous and irrational ways destroyed

The Family

everything that we had worked towards. Remembering how you would beg me to slow down and threaten to leave me, hoping that I would change my ways, only leaves me feeling that much more of a fool for not taking heeds to your advice. Which in turn has gotten me in the predicament that I am. It may seem as though it's too late to be telling you that I am sorry, but I have never gotten around to doing so in the past. I want you to go on with your life and to try to find a good man that is going to treat you and the children appropriately. I feel like so less of a man by telling you to have some other man treat my children better than I can. At times, I seriously contemplate committing suicide. The only thing that keeps me going is the hope of one-day being together with my loved ones. All that I have left in here is despair and wishful thinking. So please continue to stand by me. In these critical times I need you more now than I have ever since we've been together. You are all that I have.

I love you. Anthony.

4

The Family

This was my third letter to my wife, and it was only my third week in this hellhole. For the first two weeks in this maximum-security prison, every morning I woke up wishing that all of this shit were just a dream. But with all of these bells ringing and the screams of a man dying because he was just shanked in the back of his head with a homemade dagger, I quickly realized that this was no fucking dream. I am sitting in my cell trying to remember when all of this started.

"The beginning of the end of my life," is what I called it. It began in 1985, as I was preparing to graduate from high school. It seemed as though graduation day would never come because, instead of the usual twelve years of school needed to graduate, it took me an additional year to do so. That was due to the fact that I had fucked around one year, cutting classes and missing assignments. I did not have any definite plans in which direction my future was headed, but I was for certain that my plans would unquestionably be significantly different than those of the remaining class. Most of my classmates often talked about either going away to college or venturing into the work force. Neither one of these viewpoints struck my interest. I wanted more out of life. Some pizzazz!

Growing up in South Philadelphia in the early seventies meant that I had been exposed to the Italian Mafia, Black Incorporate, the Jamaican posses, and even the new Cambodian crip macks, originally from California. I can clearly remember the day when the infamous Angelo Bruno was gunned down in front of his home. That evening, every news station in the country must have been covering the story. Strangely, I was forever amused when I read or heard about the Italian Mafiosi wars. I was not allowed to watch such movies because I had two very strict parents who monitored my every childhood action.

My father was a trucker who drove cross-country for an Iranian marble company. If he would be home two days of the week, it would be an unusual one because he was one of the company's better drivers, which confined him to the road. Although he was on the road for a substantial amount of time he would routinely send money to my mother for our clothing and the bills. It was not a significant amount of money but it was enough to subsidize the bills and keep my tuition intact. Despite the fact that he financially maintained the family, his presence around the house was very much needed at times. It is my belief that his absence from the homefront made a considerable difference in my life and attributed to the predicament that I am currently enduring. In retrospect, my father's virtual nonexistence was supplemented with the love of my complacent mother. Everyone in the neighborhood addressed her as "mother Marge" because of the respect she commanded along with the motherly persona she upheld to the neighborhood children.

My mother was employed as a legal secretary at a downtown law firm in which she worked for eleven years. She was making good money because of her profession, and combining that with my father's income made it possible for me to attend Catholic school for twelve years. I resented going to parochial schools, wearing the same white shirt, the corresponding plaid tie, and the immutable navy blue pants day after day. The majority of children in the neighborhood went to public school and appeared to be having more fun than I was. They were allowed to do pretty much what they wanted to do by their teachers. The most significant issue was that they were able to wear everyday clothing, as well as sneakers. My mother would often explicate the distinction of being different from the norm and had frequently complimented me for looking admirable and being mild-mannered. To this day I am whole-heartedly convinced that her foremost purpose for sending me to Catholic school was for the discipline I was receiving, which ultimately would paint a brighter future for me. Later on in my adolescent years I looked down upon those who hookied school or were getting involved in drugs.

In contrast, my best friend was one of the kids from the neighborhood that other parents had banned their children from playing with. His name was Mark, an unusual kid living under extraordinary circumstances. His father was a Vietnam veteran suffering from quadriplegia. His paralysis was sustained from the hideous bloodshed in the country of

The Family

Laos during the war. In addition to returning home wheelchair bound, he had also returned a heroin addict. His last tour of duty was six months after Mark's birth, leaving his mother alone with three children. She was a good woman, but with her husband being in combat in Southeast Asia and pondering the idea of him never making it back to the states began taking its toll on her mentally. Sadly, that is probably the most logical explanation of her also getting strung out on drugs. As her addiction worsened, so did the condition of the house that they lived in. All of the utilities had been shut off and the building had become rat infested. All of these calamities occurring in such a short amount of time resulted in his mother calling it quits and leaving the kids in the care of the State Department of Human Services. Luckily for Mark, his maternal grandparents agreed to become his legal guardians and allowed him to reside in their two-story row house. Unfortunately, his siblings remained in the custody of the state. Two drug-addicted parents and Mark's brother and sister being separated from one another had made him a dejected youth.

The Family

Our back yard was adjacent to his grandparents' home and occasionally I would see him sitting on the steps playing with a make-pretend friend. One Saturday afternoon as I was playing basketball in the yard, I noticed him glumly staring at me from a window in the back of his house. Waving in his direction I gestured for him to come over to my yard and shoot around with me. When I did that I could only notice the immense grin on his face and before I could blink he had already climbed the fence and was in my yard. From that day on, a sincere friendship was established. The relationship that Mark and I shared resembled that of two long-lost brothers who were reunited after many years. Many of the other kids were not as fond of him as I was, partly because they deemed him a nerd. His clothing was outdated because it was being chosen by his grandfather, who had no sense of what style clothing was being worn amongst our peers. He often became the butt of many jokes, compliments of the neighborhood bully named JT, who received his nickname, which stood for "just talk", because that is all he ever did. Being much

10

bigger than most of us, no one dared to retaliate against him or even speak up for themselves when he started busting. Basically, he was nothing more than an asshole whose bark was bigger than his bite.

Despite what others thought of Mark he was my new best friend, and besides, I was a nerd myself and did not have many friends either. After school, we'd usually play football or watch movies resulting in a fistfight. Afterwards we would make up. During the weekends, the two of us would walk to the shopping center to pack the groceries of customers in their cars for loose change. Typically, the standard tip was in the neighborhood of twenty-five cents per customer, but occasionally we would encounter a generous shopper who tipped as much as a dollar. By mid-afternoon, the twenty-minute walk home included a stop at the grocery store to purchase sugar cookies and several cans of R.C. Colas in preparation for the kung-fu movie on channel 48.

We undertook this routine almost every weekend until we were teenagers. Mark and I deemed ourselves as an inseparable team with entrepreneurial potential. What I relished about Mark was that he had big dreams, similar to mine.

"Just because we live in the ghetto doesn't mean we have to stay here," he would sometimes say.

We were joined together at the hip. It did not stop here though, it continued all the way up until high school. It was no longer packing groceries anymore. Oh no, it got much deeper than that!

CHAPTER 2

"Weed out, Weed out!"

Dime bags of Hawaiian-grown marijuana had replaced the groceries that we used to pack in the cars of customers at the supermarket. This hustle began in the middle of our freshman year in high school. The difference between packing groceries and hustling week was, instead of us receiving twenty-five cents per customer we were getting ten dollars each transaction. Also, the partnership was no longer just Mark and I. Now we had two other friends from school that we had teamed up with named Dante and Shawn. Dante was a short stocky kid who had a complex about his height and weight. He was from the North side of the city. His family had always dealt in drugs and had also operated an exclusive numbers operation. He was a good guy, but Dante was extremely short-tempered. Because of this, his attitude had gotten us in a lot of fights when we would go to the clubs. Shawn was a half-black and Dominican who was originally from uptown Manhattan. His family had moved to

The Family

Philadelphia when he was thirteen years old. The "DA" is what we would sometimes refer to him as. He would listen to your conversation and then cross-examine the hell out of you to find out if you were sincere and telling the truth in what you were saying. Many times, even if you were telling the truth, he would make you feel like a liar anyway. This motherfucker was good! Out of all of the guys, I respected Shawn more than anyone else because he would always support anything he spoke about with common sense and logic. Having partners like this had made our business much easier to operate, as well as prosper. We had all shared the same concept; none of us was as smart as all of us.

At this point, there was not an enormous amount of profit being generated in selling weed after the four of us had to breakdown our equivalent shares. We steadily sold about three to four pounds of weed per week throughout the city because we were the only blacks who were able to maintain a consistent supply of exotic buds.

This connection was set up by me through this Italian kid named Vinny Tartaglia, with whom I had worked at the Italian Market on Ninth Street. His father, Big Vinny, was an alleged capo in the Philadelphia-New Jersey based Mafia who had received a life sentence for murder and racketeering charges. Before his conviction he was the main supplier of methamphetamine, cocaine, and marijuana, importing to the tri-state area via the waterfronts. So, quite naturally, the business was then handed down to little Vinny. He and I had always had a candid respect for one another. I was not intimidated by his family's power or their friends simply because they were in the mob, because in my eyes they were still white boys and that was the bottom line.

Selling pounds of weed per week was proper, but we began growing impatient for faster and more substantial money. Mark had mentioned the idea of selling cocaine, but at the time of that discussion we did not have a sufficient amount of money to purchase an ample amount of blow, which in turn could have been resold on the streets. In the late 70s going in to the early 80s, cocaine was considered to be a rich man's high, so that

15

meant that the cost of it, even on a wholesale rate, was going to be mad expensive. Besides the soaring prices of the shit, we also did not have a clientele to whom the shit could have been sold.

Right now, the times were a little different from when we had that first conversation. We had now made some money and by dealing with an older crowd of weedheads, we had met some of their friends who had happened to do coke as well. Now was a good time to make a move, but Vinny was the only person that we knew that we could have purchased some weight from. We needed to concoct a plan on how this idea could be carried out, and how we could find an alternate supplier. Make no mistake, Vinny and his boys did not treat us well, but in this business, when a supplier realizes that he is your only option, they tend to ante up the prices of shit more than necessary. We had arranged a meeting to be held on a Saturday night preceding a rap show at the After Midnite club in Center City. The meeting was going to be held in the Penns Landing area, a tranquil section that bordered the waterfront where many illegal activities were carried out.

The After Midnite club was a new joint that had featured the hottest disk jockeys and M.C.'s from Philadelphia and New York. Occasionally, there would be other rap groups from Washington, DC and California that would come to perform. This particular evening, on the same night we were scheduled to have our meeting, the club was having the 1985 high school class salute. The show was going to be for all of the graduating high school classes for that year. Highlighting the show was going to be new rapper from New York by the name of L.L. Cool J. Prior to this show no one ever heard of this guy, but from all the talk that was going on, he was supposed to be the shit in New York because he had mad rhyming skills. The club had always featured up and coming artists, but on the same note, on any given weekend, you could still see the Ultra Magnetic M.C.'s, Salt 'n Pepa, or hear two M.C.'s battling, such as the legendary Big Daddy Kane versus Jazz Fresh, who was a local Philly legend. The night was off the hook with L.L. Cool J.

freestyling over the "It's Yours" track by TLA ROCK.

The show was not the only memorable event that happened that evening, because it was also the same night that we were going to concoct a scheme on how we were going to produce more abundant capital by substituting the marijuana for cocaine. Superseding the drugs was not the only change we needed, but also our ideology had to be converted; we needed to broaden our horizons, so to speak. I had envisioned us as not being classified as a group of thugs selling drugs, but rather as a close-knit organization with influential connections, more or less emulating the Italians.

At the meeting, the first topic of conversation was what was going to be the designated roles of each one of us in this alliance. Shawn had suggested that the most adequate manner in handling this dilemma would be for the four of us to have an equal amount of authority with no one of us having more say so than another. This designed structure was to maintain the equilibrium amongst four delegates where our individual egos would not interfere with the good of our intentions. It took us about two hours of deliberating on how we were going to distribute the cocaine as well as a methodical way of eliminating our potential competition. As far as the potential competitors were concerned, there were no other organized gangs that we would have to contend with other than the vast, expanding Jamaican posses. The script was simple: outdo our competition by supplying the demand with a better quality of cocaine. Our ultimate goal was to eventually have all of the motherfuckers that were dealing coke either working for us or being supplied by us. There were not going to be any exceptions to this rule. "Be good or be gone," was the motto that was later on associated with my team by everyone here in the city.

Dante had raised a very good point in stating that we did not have another connection other than Vinny. Mark had then made us aware that he had befriended a kid named June whom he had met while locked up in a juvenile hall. He said June was a Dominican boy that was from Manhattan's

The Family

Washington Heights section, who had worked as a mule for some Colombian drug traffickers, whose base of operations was located in the Miami Beach area, but had extended to Philadelphia, New York, Chicago, and as far as Los Angeles. June had gotten arrested at the 30th Street Amtrak station attempting to deliver two hundred and fifty two grams of cocaine to an informant that had been doing business with his boss. He had spent approximately two years in the lockup facility where he had met my man Mark.

Before he had gotten released he had told Mark that when he got out of jail he was going to move to Florida and that if he ever needed anything that he would be there for him. June had felt compelled to look out for him because Mark had done the same thing for him during the years that they were institutionalized together. Mark said he had June's phone number somewhere in the house and tomorrow he would attempt to look for it.

Now, with everything being said, the meeting had been concluded. We had all left the meeting with an assured vote of confidence that what we were planning to undertake could in fact work out, as long as everyone stuck to the game plan.

Two days later Mark found the telephone number and informed us to meet him at his house at the time he was going to make the phone call. The next day, when I reached his home, he told me that Shawn and Dante had bumped into an old acquaintance named Maurice, who was from North Carolina. He had just arrived in town trying to sell a couple of guns that he had bought down South. He told them that he had made connections with some artillery in Raleigh, and if we wanted a thorough hookup on some gats, that it could be arranged by him. The Carolinas has always been known for inexpensive tooleys that were just as easy to purchase in a gun store as on the streets.

It just so happened that at this particular stage in our plans, guns were going to be a must, considering the shit that we were set to begin. So Shawn and Dante took the eight-hour trip down South in search of a good deal on some heaters. In the meantime, Mark had called June's crib but had only received an answering machine with June's voice on it.

The Family

He had left his name and phone number on the answering service and a message for June to contact him as soon as possible.

While waiting for June's returned phone call, Mark and I drove to Russell Street to pick up a couple bags of killer and then headed to the Plateau. As we listened to DJ Cosmic Kev and Jazzy Jeff battling on the turntables, Mark expressed his feelings towards me. He reminded me of how I had been such a good friend to him since he had moved into the neighborhood. He also spoke of his fucked up childhood and how if what we were putting together worked out, that it could make him feel like a normal person. I knew exactly what he was getting at, because growing up together I had witnessed a lot of the bullshit that he had gone through. By making money he figured others would accept him. It is said that money can't buy happiness, but it damn sure can help.

After he stated what was on his mind, I reminded him that even though we were a team composed of four people, that it was mainly up to me and him to step up and be the big dogs of this shit. It was my belief that we would have to rule with an iron fist and make those that were around us think like we did. That concept was based on the theory that states, "when you control a man's thinking, you do not have to worry about his actions."

We had kicked it for a little while longer before returning to Mark's house to see if June had called. As we reached the front of Mark's door his answering machine could be heard recording a message. By the time he had stopped fiddling with his key, trying to open the jammed lock, the message had ended. Once we had gotten in the house, Mark rewound the tape and played the message:

"Mark, what's up bro? This is June. I'm returning your phone call that I received earlier today. I'm going to be in Fort Lauderdale for all of the day tomorrow, so you can give me a call at area code 954-555-2781. Peace."

That was the phone call we had been waiting for all day. But we decided that we would call June back the next day when Shawn and Dante were supposed to be back from Raleigh.

The Family

They returned the next morning at about ten o'clock, with terrific news. The long trip was well worth it because they were able to purchase three German-made Luger nine millimeter hand guns, a rare Russian made glock 45, and two AK-47s with banana clips, all for the low price of twelve hundred dollars. Up North, these same guns could have cost us about thirty-five hundred dollars. We informed them of the returned phone call from June and that we were going to give him a call in the early afternoon. Shawn advised us that it would be more prudent to place the phone call at a pay phone as opposed to calling from the house, just in case either of our phone lines were tapped.

As Mark placed the phone call at the phone booth on the corner of his block, we stood on the opposite side of the street talking to some girls from the neighborhood named Atiyya and Lauryn. Lauryn was a girl that I had been trying to get with for years, but she had always been the type of female who was more into her books than she was into boys. She and I talked for awhile before her father drove up and made her get into the car. Her pop did not like her talking to the neighborhood guys because he felt as though we weren't about shit, and that his daughter undoubtedly deserved better. I had glanced across the street noticing that Mark had engaged in an intricate conversation with whoever he was on the phone. The conversation went on for about fifteen more minutes before he hung up and walked across the street.

"Who is the man, motherfuckers?" he jokingly said.

"Man, fuck all that," Dante responded with a frown. "What did June say, Mark?"

He said that he was running mad shit in the Dade and Broward counties, and if we came to Florida to get with him, he will personally see to it that we would be taken care of."

"June sounded like he was shining like a real big boy," Mark said, while rolling up some weed.

We had decided that Mark and I were going to fly to Miami while Shawn and Dante remained in Philly until they received word from us to Western Union the money.

Everything was going as planned. From this period on I had referred to it as the

The Family

'Philadelphia Renaissance Era' because it seemed as though everyone was shining. Selling drugs had become the most popular way to make a living amongst the urban young. There was no difference between other drug dealers and us in the city. We were all hustlers on the same journey. My team just had better road maps.

CHAPTER 3

I woke up at six-thirty in the morning to begin packing my clothes for our scheduled trip to Florida to meet with June. Lauryn had made the reservations for us and had paid for the airline tickets on her credit card. She and I had secretly begun seeing each other without her parents' awareness for about a month. She would lie to her folks by telling them that she was spending the night over at her girlfriend Erykahs' house, just so she could be with me. My feelings for Lauryn had now grown deeper as did my trust for her. She was not the flyest girl in the neighborhood, or even the prettiest for that matter, but she was mine and had become my best friend as well. Many nights we would sit in the park holding hands, reminiscing about when we were little kids and how we were going to make a lot of money and then move down South. She had just graduated high school and planned on attending Norfolk State University in Virginia, but I had convinced her to stay here with me and go to school the following semester. It was selfish of me to delay her ambitions, but, like most drug dealers, I thought my aspirations of ghetto glory were more significant.

Initially, Lauryn was in total disagreement with me going to Florida, but she had a change of heart once she had realized that this venture was not just about my personal well being, but rather a step closer to a brighter future for both of us. While driving to the airport I stopped at a nearby florist and purchased a dozen black roses and had them delivered to her job.

Our flight departed from Philadelphia promptly at eleven-thirty in the morning and landed in Miami at two o'clock in the afternoon. By this time the temperature had already reached the upper nineties and the humidity made it feel as though it was over a hundred. We were not able to rent a car because you had to be 25 or older with a major credit card, so we flagged down a taxi and instructed him to drive us to the downtown Miami Beach area, where we could find a hotel to stay in.

Mark and I noticed, while driving through the Miami Beach area, that there was a heavy influence of Spaniards and West Indians throughout the city. Back in Philly we were mainly exposed only to Puerto Ricans and a handful of Jamaicans, but Miami appeared to be a melting pot of diverse cultures along the East Coast. We rented a hotel room located on Collins Avenue that cost twenty-five dollars per night and was furnished with a stove, television, and two beds. Mark suggested that we spend the rest of the day relaxing and give his friend June a call in the early afternoon of the next day. The rest of the day was spent on the beach smoking weed, and tripping off all of the olive-skinned Latin women that were switching their cute little asses around in thongs.

Later that evening, the weather changed and became moderate with a stirring breeze. I returned to the hotel and put on a sweatshirt and a pair of jeans. Meanwhile, Mark remained at an outdoor beach restaurant talking with a Trinidadian girl he had met earlier in the day. While changing my clothes, I began to think of Lauryn and how much I already missed her. I decided to call her before leaving the room to head back and meet Mark. Ironically, when I called her, she told me she was just thinking about me, and that she had waited in the house all day for my phone call.

"Why did it take you all of the day to call me, baby?" she questioned.

"Because Mark and I were on the beach for a little while swimming," I laughingly replied.

"Yeah, I bet, nigga," she replied sarcastically. "You and Mark were probably on the beach looking at other bitches!"

Lauryn was becoming increasingly jealous with me, but I honestly did not mind because I had become the same way with her as well. She pleaded with me not to go outside and to stay on the phone with her for a little while longer. I agreed to do so but only if she would talk dirty to me, and express how much she missed me. Moments before we were about to hang up, she promised that we were going to make love for the first time upon me arriving back home. She really caught me off guard when she began telling me of her impetuous desires, because I had wrongfully assumed the intimate aspect of our relationship was going to be procrastinated because of her being a virgin. She had begun detailing what our passionate evening was going to consist of doing, but before she was able to conclude with her passionate chimera, the twisting of the doorknob could be heard. Mark entered the room. I told Lauryn that I would call her tomorrow in the early afternoon.

Up the next morning, our day began with a continental breakfast at a fancy hotel on the boardwalk. After breakfast we devised our detail in which manner we were going to contrive our proposition with June. By the time we had completed eating our breakfast the afternoon was nearing. The meeting with June was scheduled at one o'clock. We had an hour to waste before our confabulation. To kill some time, Mark and I walked along the beach, trudging through the sand, collecting seashells and admiring the beautiful ladies tanning. About 12:45 we left the beach and flagged down a taxi and instructed him to drive us to the Biscayne Bridge where June had told us to meet him at one o'clock sharp. Upon reaching our destination, June was accompanied by three other older Hispanic men.

"¿Que pasa?" June said as he reached out to shake Mark's hand. "Long time, no see."

"This is my friend Ant," Mark said as he formally introduced me.

"These are my three bosses," June replied. "They do not speak English," June said while pointing, "but I will translate our conversation for them, and besides I have already told them about you guys coming to Florida."

I began to feel slightly uncomfortable because the older men just stared at us without uttering a word while June and Mark began speaking.

"June, this is the deal," Mark voiced as he began walking away from the men. "Me and several of my boys are attempting to organize a massive drug ring back in Philly and to do so we would need an out-of-state, reasonable cocaine connection. And that is why we are attempting to link up with you and your boys.

"You came to the right source," said June while draping his arms around Mark's neck. "How much money are you guys working with?"

"Fifteen thousand dollars," Mark quickly responded.

"You know, bro, prices here in Florida are much cheaper than they are up North," June uttered.

"No shit, Sherlock," Mark sarcastically replied.

"Well, let me talk it over with my bosses and see if I could possibly get a better deal than the norm. Hold on for a minute."

June flagged the men and the four of them began speaking Spanish. The conversation lasted for about five minutes before June returned to us.

"My bosses said since you guys are friends of mine, they agreed to give you two kilos for the fifteen thousand dollars, and you guys owe us an additional five thousand dollars on the next deal."

Mark and I stared at each other in a state of disbelief because we could not believe what we just heard.

"You are going to give us two keys for fifteen thousand and we owe you five thousand dollars?" Mark reiterated.

"Yeah, Mark, that is the best that we can do right now. But as time goes on and we build a level of trust, who knows what could happen," June assured him.

"That's a bet," Mark responded. "We are going to need at least a couple of hours before we can give you the money because it is going to be Western Unioned," he added.

"That's cool," June replied. "Give me the address of your hotel and I will have the material delivered to you as early as ten o'clock in the morning."

As Mark and I drove back to the hotel in the taxi we discussed the advantages of the agreement that was rendered by June and his bosses.

"Ant, do you realize that we are getting kilos for ten thousand dollars apiece?" Mark emphatically questioned. "That is half of the price they are selling for up North, kid. And plus the quality of the shit is probably close to 90 percent pure compared to the bullshit that is being cut up and resold by the dagos in Philly."

I was so overwhelmed by how unerringly our negotiations had gone that I was left awestruck. The only thought that could be conceived at the time was that of money.

The Family

Before reaching the hotel we stopped at the Western Union office, which was a couple of blocks from our hotel, to contact Shawn and Dante. We told them the aspects of our deal and to send the money.

The rest of the day was spent shopping at clothing stores. Later on in the evening we visited Luke's, a slamming ass club that was owned by the rapper. Despite all of the half-dressed women that were in the joint I could not really enjoy myself because I was thinking of my baby Lauryn who remained in Philly, waiting for me to come back. We left the club at about four o'clock in the morning with Mark bringing a beautiful Panamanian girl he met back to the room. Before going to sleep I called Lauryn only to receive an answering machine.

The next morning, we were awakened by the phone ringing. The operator at the front desk informed us that we had two guests waiting in the lobby of the hotel. Mark instructed her to direct them to our room. June arrived with two beautiful Hispanic girls and a large Eddie Bauer traveling bag containing neatly wrapped squared bricks of

The Family

cocaine. As June and Mark talked, me and the two women began counting the money. Looking on the outside of the two neatly wrapped bricks; shiny fish-like scales could be seen shining through the clear plastic. Everything went as planned with the deal ending in a handshake, as the three exited the room. Mark instructed me to contact Greyhound to find out the schedule for departing buses arriving in Philadelphia.

The earliest bus leaving from Miami and arriving in Philly was scheduled to leave at seven o'clock in the morning. We packed our belongings and prepared for our departure. Traveling on the bus was doomed to be very uncomfortable and time-consuming. But in retrospect it was safe and that was most important. Arriving at the bus terminal our suitcases were placed in the undercarriage of the bus, while the drugs were placed in the overhead compartment. Mark sat in the front of the bus and I settled in the rear of the bus. Travel time was 29 hours with one layover in Fayetteville, North Carolina. I reclined in the uncomfortable seat with my Walkman,

The Family

listening to a Clue mix-tape and prepared for
the long ride home.

The Family

CHAPTER 4

"Last stop, Philadelphia," hollered the red-eyed bus driver."

The 29-hour commute back to the city had finally come to an end with Dante and Shawn awaiting our return at the terminal. Despite travel time, our method of transporting proved to be effective as well as safe. An old-time gangster who we only knew as Sam had advised us that the more local you maintain interstate transportation, the less likely you were to get jammed. The lack of communication by the local and federal authorities made it almost impossible to keep track of potential traffickers.

Shawn rented a hotel suite near the airport so we could break down the coke and prudently outline a distribution plan. Since we had two kilos and owed June five grand, Mark wisely suggested that at least one of the kilos be sold entirely in the lowest denominations, which were twenty-dollar bags. Uncut. This would ensure a significant profit, an expeditious payment of our tab, and superior quality of material for our clientele.

As for the other brick, that would be sold in measures of weighs such as quarter ounces, halves, and quarter pounds. Predicting an enormous amount of attention by other dealers, as a result of us selling uncut twenties, one could rightfully assume that jealousy would become an inevitable demeanor. Wholesaling weight to competition was a clever method of regulating their business and a tactic to maintain the peace. Mark and I began breaking the first brick into twenties while Shawn and Dante weighed the other by seven grams per baggy.

From the kilo that was being bagged as twenties we netted $54,000, on account of each one of the thirty-six ounces grossing fifteen hundred dollars apiece. The kilo we sold to other dealers at $600 per ounce wholesale price generated an additional $21,600. The total gross amounted to $75,600, which was not bad for a twenty thousand-dollar investment. Incidentally, the wholesale price of ounces here in the city ranged from $800 to $1200. That meant we would be cutting other costs by as much as fifty percent, which would undoubtedly raise

40

the eyebrows of the any dealer who wanted to stay in business. The grueling process of bagging all this shit took well over twelve hours, so we decided to keep the room for an additional day.

Before calling it quits for the night, I phoned Lauryn to notify her that I was back in town. She had a fit because I had not called her in almost two days. Not giving much thought to her feelings should have been a subliminal indication that our lifestyle had begun to change without notice. Her fussing would never last long, because whenever I would get myself in a jam I would make her laugh to pacify the situation. You know you can't stay mad at someone who makes you laugh. Before we hung up the telephone she told me that her pussy was throbbing and the juices from her lips were now seeping through her scanty lace panties that she was wearing.

By listening to her verbal orgasm I developed an erection myself, and suggested we get a hotel room for the weekend. She enthusiastically agreed. Having my lady in my corner, Dante, Shawn, and Mark on my

41

team, and nearly eighty thousand dollars, made me feel like a Don, you know?

Everything was bagged up; so the only scenario left to orchestrate were our distribution plans, which were going to be revealed by Shawn in the morning. He had concocted a distribution scheme while we were connecting with June and his boys in Florida. Everyone overslept and did not awake until hearing a knock on the door from room service. We ordered lunch and then Shawn began detailing the plan.

"Check it out, y'all, this is what we're going to do," he said as he began explaining. "We are going to set four corners up with hand-to-hand sales, directly to the customer, selling the twenty dollar bags."

"I have two locations in the Spanish part of North Philly," he further explained, "one at Eighth and Butler Streets, and the other at Fifth and Indiana Avenue." (Incidentally, these two corners would later become the two most notorious streets in Philadelphia, and the first to feature open-air trafficking.)

"I also got 52nd and Market Street and Seventh and Snyder Avenue in motion," he continued. "Now from a strategic marketing outlook, we will pretty much cover most of the city as far as the cokeheads are concerned, but also, we are cutting the pockets of other dealers in that neighborhood. With that being a fact, they would ultimately have to hook up with us or get the fuck out of the game."

The three of us could only stare at Shawn as he continued speaking because who could honestly believe he could devise a strategy so simple but effective? Not to discredit his intelligence, but this shit was brilliant.

"I got a question," Mark announced. "How in the fuck are we going to operate in Puerto Rican territory in North Philly and the Jamaican area in West Philly without those kids catching feelings?"

"Oh, that's simple," Shawn replied. "I have these two Puerto Rican boys named Angelo and Spel who we are going to pay to operate the two corners. Sort of like caseworkers, you know? Now see," he further explained, "with having two Ricans running the show down there, most people will believe it is their shit and be less likely to stir any trouble. Get it?"

The Family

"I got you," Mark answered, holding his head.

"Its not like we are going in this like bitches, but we are going to take the comment of the U.S. drug czar into consideration. He stated that violent drug gangs don't last long and take heed by being as nonviolent as possible. As far as the Jamaicans are concerned, we will have to cross that bridge when we get there, because you know those cowboys won't take "no" for an answer. So, with this, gentlemen, our meeting is adjourned," Shawn stated as he stood up stretching. We left the hotel. Mark and I left with the weight, and Shawn and Dante bounced the other direction with the twenties.

The rest of the day I spent unpacking my clothes and later that evening Lauryn and I took the train to New York to visit her cousin Inga and her boyfriend. The four of us went to see Lean On Me, then had dinner later on at Cheffy's, a popular Jamaican restaurant located in Brooklyn on Nostrand Avenue. Lauryn wanted us to spend the night at Inga's house, but I told her I had important business to tend to in the morning. I said I would make it up to her over the weekend during our stay at the hotel. Inga's boyfriend Nasir agreed to drive us to the bus terminal on Forty-Second Street.

As we were driving on the West Side Highway, the back tire of the car suddenly blew out. While Inga steered the car, we both pushed it alongside the guardrails and began fixing the flat. We laughed all the way to the bus station about this embarrassing shit.

I took a particular liking to Nasir and Inga because we shared many camaraderie's, judging by the little time the four of us spent together. Nasir, like me, was trying to establish himself in the game in his neighborhood of Queens. He was unable to do so because of a group of older cats that had the borough on lockdown. We exchanged phone numbers before we left, and I told him I would contact him if anything were to come up. We arrived in Philly at two-thirty in the morning and took a taxi to South Philly.

Before meeting the boys the next day I walked to old head Sam's house to get a few words from him and to seek his opinion on this matter. He was a tall, light-skinned

45

brother who had an unusually muscular build for a middle-aged man. As he opened the door, the shining of what appeared to be a .38 could be seen wedged between his shirt and pants.

"What's up, little brother?" he greeted.

After making him aware of what we were doing he gave me several suggestions of what he thought would keep us in business.

"First of all," he explained, "do not start buying a whole bunch of jewelry and cars once you start getting that money. That is what fucked up a whole lot of brothers. Also, remember to clean some of that dirty money by investing it back into the neighborhood. You will be surprised how many of those other neighbors who called the cops on other motherfuckers protect your black ass because they know if you go down, so will the community. The Italians have been doing that shit for years. And last, little brother, manipulate politicians by contributing to their campaigns."

"Politicians?" I questioned.

"You're goddamned right," he emphatically answered. "Look, those

46

cocksuckers make the laws so you know damn well they can twist and bend that shit when need be. And the type of business you're in, you're going to need all the fucking political influence you can get. In that game, you win some and you lose some, and then the game is over."

The more Sam spoke the louder his voice rose and the more agitated he seemed to become. I believe he was pondering the thought of how he and his cronies fell off, and that made him react this way. Before he continued his lecture, I reassured him that I would bear in mind his advice and pass it on to the fellas.

Traveling across town by way of taxi with over thirty thousand dollars in cocaine made me incredibly paranoid, but the others maintained their cool. Our first stop was on the second floor atop a Spanish restaurant on Indiana Avenue where Spel and Angelo told us they'd be waiting for us. They received precise instructions to divide half of the seventeen thousand dollars in twenties and distribute them between the two corners according to the demand. In addition, every

The Family

thousand dollars sold was immediately to be turned in by way of Mark or Shawn.

"How much are we going to get paid, bro?" questioned Spel.

"Y'all are going to start off by getting paid five hundred dollars per week, but as the corners grow, so will your salary," assured Mark. "That's a bet, or what?"

The two agreed and left the room with the dope. We packed up the other half of the drugs and headed to Market Street, then Snyder Avenue. Following the same system we instituted in North Philly we emulated a very similar pattern in the other two sections. Now all of the legwork was completed and the only thing for us to do was to wait and begin collecting our money.

CHAPTER 5

Sixty-six thousand and six hundred dollars is what was netted after two and a half weeks of being in business. Our debt of five thousand dollars owed to June was immediately Western Unioned to him upon selling the equivalent of cocaine. Also, an additional four thousand dollars was paid to the workers who diligently labored on the corners to establish our reputation. The word not only spread among customers but it permeated amidst other dealers in the city also. Angelo and Spel informed us that on many nights the demand would become so great that as many as twenty cars would be lined up, as if it were the checkout line at the supermarket. We received corresponding reactions from Maurice and Big Tone, who established the South and West Philly corners. After three or four days of diminishing sales, other hustlers asked our street boys about purchasing wholesale quantities. We were not reluctant in doing so because their business inevitably would then be regulated by ours, making them incapable of being legitimate competitors. Meanwhile, a meeting at the Marriott was called to count our money and discuss further plans.

"Ant, we are going to leave the decision up to you as to how we should cop from this point on," Mark said. The guys designating me to officiate our purchasing plan made me feel important and drove my self-esteem up to the ceiling. Before making a decision, I recalled a conversation Sam and I partook in wherein he stressed reaching a goal before deciding to buy jewelry and cars.

"Look, y'all, we are trying to build something for the future, so I think it's only right to invest at least fifty thousand and the remainder of the profit can be divided by the four of us. How does that sound?"

Everyone agreed.

"So, Mark, you should contact June to let him know that we will be in Miami by tomorrow evening and to pick us up at the Airport. In the meantime, Dante and Shawn, let everyone know that we'll be back in effect within two days."

The Family

"How about if me and Shawn cop a big eight from Vinny to maintain the flow until you guys return?" suggested Dante.

"That's a good idea, because we wouldn't want to lose any money while we are gone," I contended. "That's everything, right? Let's be out."

"Oh, one last thing, Shawn and Dante: If Vinny asks you about what we are doing or where we're at, don't tell him shit. It is none of his fucking business."

I told them to say that because I knew if Vinny found out how lucrative our business was becoming, he probably would notify his people to issue a street tax. And we weren't prepared to go to war. Not yet anyway.

The next morning before leaving for the airport Lauryn called to tell me she was coming over to say a few things she had on her mind. The very minute I opened the door to allow her in, I knew by her facial expression that an argument was imminent.

"Ant, before you open your mouth to say some dumb shit, where have you been and why the fuck haven't you been calling me?" she said while pointing.

51

The Family

"Lauryn, look, I'm sorry but I've been busy as hell for the past two weeks."

"Busy?" she questioned while rolling her eyes. "You mean to tell me you been that busy you couldn't have picked up the telephone to call me? You know I do not want you into that type of stuff because you can go to jail or get killed," she continued. "And furthermore, it is already messing up our relationship."

"Messing up our relationship, Lauryn? Because I can't call you for a couple of day's means our relationship is messed up? I don't understand that."

"Well what about last weekend when you were supposed to rent us a room and spend the weekend with me? You just forgot all about that, right?"

"Look, Lauryn, this shit is for the birds. I have an airplane to catch and I'll talk to you when I get home."

"Don't just walk away from me while I'm talking to you," she said while grabbing my shoulder.

The Family

"Hey, girl, don't make me put my hands on you. Didn't I tell you I'll talk to you when I get back?"

"I won't be here for you when you get back," she emphasized while slamming the door.

Up to this point, everything was going fine until she started bitching, but deep inside I knew she was right in what she was saying, so I couldn't be upset with her. There was no turning back now; I'd have to make it up to her when I returned.

Suddenly, a horn blew from outside and Mark's voice could be heard shouting my name. I began loading the cab with my belongings and the money in suitcases. The driver pulled off. As he was nearing the corner Lauryn was standing they're talking to her girlfriend. I attempted to say something through the window but before I could say a word she stuck up her middle finger and turned her back. Fuck it! I said to myself. I put my head on the seat, closed my eyes, and napped until we reached the airport.

As the airplane flew through the picturesque skyline, I began thinking about how my life had suddenly changed so much in such a little amount of time. All the years of Catholic education meant absolutely nothing because I had become the same self-destructive toxin of the hood, similar to those I used to despise and look down upon. The only justification for these demeanors was the rationalization that white America was not going to give me the opportunity to achieve anything, and that is the sole reason for me doing what I was doing. I wanted the finer attributes of life, and I refused to endure the adversities sanctioned upon my grandparents in the South. Furthermore, I spurned attending college to acquire the craft of ass kissing and behaving as an Uncle Tom in corporate America.

The only way of predicting the future was by creating it. So building upon this theory I put on my headphones, listened to a Funk Master Flex tape, closed my eyes and eagerly waited to land in Florida.

June met us at the airport, then drove to a remote area in Fort Lauderdale. The house we journeyed to was immaculate. It was a 46-acre gothic building with two Olympic-sized pools, imported marble floors, a newly built stable surrounded by a manmade lake with tropical fish. From the moment we entered the premises my heart started racing and my lips quivered because never had I been in such a place that was so beautiful. Here were two city kids used to living in row houses all their lives now in the company of millionaires inside of a chateau.

"You guys are moving kind of fast," stated June, while fixing martinis. "Faster than what I anticipated," he continued. "And because of that, gentlemen, me and the bosses have some big plans for you guys. Big plans." The three of us continued talking before hearing a car pull up into the driveway. "That's my bosses. Guys, excuse me for a second," he explained while walking to open the door. Three men walked over to us, shaking our hands and speaking Spanish as if we understood.

"¿Que. pass, amigos?" one of the older men said.

"He said 'what's up?'" June smilingly translated.

"Sientate por favor," the man voiced while motioning his hand toward a beauteous settee.

55

The Family

Mark and I looked at one another because, once again, we could not interpret what was said.

"'Please sit down' is what he said," June once again translated. "This is Don Delgado, Señor Martinez, and Señor Antonio Cruz," he introduced. "My bosses recognized how quickly the material was sold and the debt repaid and which to effect a marriage between our organizations. We're a vast group that is expanding along the East and West Coast, with restaurants, car dealerships, social organizations, and very strong ties to the Spanish communities.

"It would be in our best interest to see that the brothers are embraced. For years the Italians, Greeks, and the Jews have been privileged to enjoy the fruits of our labor, and now it is our time to get a piece of the pie. I don't know how much money you guys came with but if you would accept the generous offer proposed by my bosses, you would find this journey the most significant expedition of your lives."

"What is the proposition?" Mark asked.

The Family

"How much money did you guys bring to be invested?"

"Fifty thousand dollars," I answered.

"Cincuenta Mel Deneros," he translated to the bosses.

For a moment he paused. "For the fifty thousand dollars you can purchase ten kilos, and we are going to advance an additional ninety squares for forty-five thousand dollars. Do you think that would be equitable?" June queried.

"It sounds good to me," I replied.

"Well, if everyone agrees to these terms," June commented. "It's a done deal."

"Bienvenido a la familia," Don Delgado expressed while shaking our hands.

June took the money and walked to the back of the estate. He then indicated for us to remain placid for a few minutes.

Twenty minutes passed before June and his cronies returned with ten suitcases.

"Here is everything, guys," he said upon returning. "I have arranged for two girls along with Señor Antonio Cruz to have the rest of the material waiting for you guys by the time you reach Philadelphia. Here is the address of

The Family

restaurant we own in Far Rockaway, Queens. Mr. Cruz is a prominent businessman in that area so you shouldn't have any problems with the policia. Once you arrive in Philly contact Cheryl and Sandy, two beautiful girls who operate a modeling agency for us. Let them know you are affiliated with us and they'll know what to do.

"Guys, your ride should be arriving shortly to escort you to the airport."

The three men left the estate while June, Mark, and I loitered in the driveway. The stretch Lincoln Town Car pulled alongside of the entrance and the driver packed our belongings in the trunk of the limousine. Before leaving June tapped on the window of the tinted glass and spoke his last words.

"This is an opportunity of a lifetime, so let's keep everything legit. The first time you fuck us will be the last. Son solo negocios, nada personal," he expressed in Spanish. "It is only business, nothing personal."

We then headed to the airport.

CHAPTER 6

"Show Stoppers Modeling Agency. How may I help you?"

"Hi, How are you doing? My name is Anthony, may I speak with Cheryl or Sandy?"

"Please hold," the female receptionist said.

I was kept on hold for a couple of minutes before a woman with a sensual voice answered.

"This is Cheryl, how may I help you?"

"Hi, Cheryl. This is Anthony from Philadelphia," I replied.

"Hey, what's up?" she yelled while picking up the receiver taking me off the speakerphone. "I have spoken with Mr. Cruz, and I will be meeting you guys at the Travelodge hotel in Mount Laurel, New Jersey, tomorrow at ten o'clock sharp. The room number is suite 1507, okay baby?" she rushingly said.

"All right then, Cheryl. We'll see you," I responded before hanging up the phone.

The conversation went by so fast that I was unable to ask her for directions to get to Mount Laurel. Mount Laurel was not that far

The Family

from Philly so I did not prognosticate having too much of a problem finding the place with help from the other guys. Later that night Mark, Shawn, and Dante went to a 76ers game while Lauryn and I stayed at a hotel for the evening. I promised to spend more time with her when I came back so I kept my word. The next morning arrived with the boys picking me up at the hotel with a rented U-Haul truck. I gave Lauryn five hundred dollars to catch a taxi home and later to go to Caesar's Palace in Atlantic City to get us a pair of Gucci sneakers.

"Be careful, baby, and I love you," she said to me while blowing a kiss getting into the taxi."

"Who are these bitches we are supposed to be meeting in New Jersey?" Shawn questioned.

"They ain't no bitches," replied Mark. "They are two girls who work for the Colombians that operate a modeling agency in New York."

"Suppose these bitches are setting us up?" Shawn stupidly questioned.

"Setting us up for what, dickhead?" Mark answered. "You ain't nobody, motherfucker, so shut the hell up and enjoy the ride."

Once we arrived at the Travelodge, two fine sisters dressed in business-like attire answered the door. "Y'all must be the guys from Philly," the well-figured, light-skinned sister said. "Here are the keys for the truck that is parked adjacent to the red Mercedes car with the New Jersey license plates. The material is properly stored in the fruit baskets in the rear of the truck."

After saying that, the two of them walked to the Mercedes, waited for us to pull off, then drove in the opposite direction. Shawn and Dante drove the truck with the cocaine in it while Mark and I followed immediately behind them. The reason for us following directly behind them was to avoid tailgating by the highway police. Once crossing the Walt Whitman Bridge, we continued on I-95 north to the Northeast section of Philadelphia. Where Shawn and Dante had rented an apartment, so we could allocate and stockpile our goods. Spel, Angelo, Big Tone, and

Maurice were already at the house and began unloading the crates when we arrived.

"What the fuck is all of the shit?" Angelo questioned.

"I'll tell you guys later," I replied. "Just unload everything and park the truck in the back."

We counted all the kilos, which totaled to 110 bricks, ten more than there was supposed to be.

"Oh shit, we got ten extra keys for ourselves," Dante excitedly said.

"No, you dumb fuck," I rebutted. "You did not make a mistake with ten keys, this is just a test of our honesty."

"Mark, immediately contact Señor Cruz to make him aware of this mistake," I instructed. "Let me know what he says."

Mark returned to say that Mr. Cruz apologized for the honest mistake and as a gesture of good will to keep the extra for ourselves.

"See? I told you so," I explained. They were only scrutinizing our principles."

"How are we going to distribute all of this?" Dante wondered.

"Fifty of the kilos are going to be bagged in twenties, but double the size as the last time, the other fifty kilos are going to be wholesaled," I said.

"How about the additional ten kilos that were given by Mr. Cruz?" Mark questioned.

"We all take two apiece for ourselves and save the other two as a backup in case of an emergency," Dante explained. "Let's start bagging, boys."

It took us over forty-eight grueling hours to bag up all of the shit. The total was one point eight million dollars in twenty dollar bags and seven hundred and fifty thousand dollars of wholesale material if we sold each kilo for fifteen thousand dollars to other dealers. That excluded the other two kilos we each had a piece of from the over-shipped delivery. Selling all of this dope would make us immediate millionaires. But with everything going so fast, I did not realize how well to do we'd become.

Big Tone, Maurice, Spel, and Angelo no longer worked on the corners. They were made street bosses in charge of collecting money, delivering material and reporting directly to us. They checked the corners, we checked them and the Colombians checked us. We were now one big family. After a week of the material being on the street the whole city was in an uproar. No one had ever seen the quality or quantity of cocaine that was now flooding the streets of Philadelphia. Other dealers never knew the source of the supply, the law had no idea of any connection and the junkies were happy.

We made forty-five thousand in the first week and immediately drove the money to New York to Mr. Cruz. He said it was safer to bring the money to New York as opposed to Western Union it to Miami. During the weekend, the eight of us drove to Albany, New York where Don Delgado owned a car dealership to purchase new cars. Me, Mark, Dante and Shawn bought late-model convertible Ford mustangs equipped with telephones. Tone, Spel, Angelo, and Maurice bought kitted-up Audio 5000s. The sight of eight brand new cars turned the heads of everyone traveling on the expressway that evening. We drove around the city showing off our new whips and acting like big boys.

The Family

The next day, Lauryn and I drove to New York to visit Inga and Nasir and go shopping in Manhattan. We met them at Port Authority on Forty-second Street, then headed to Bloomingdale's.

"Damn, nigga, you came up," Nasir said. "Where did you get this fly ass car from, kid?" he questioned.

"We'll talk," I explained to him.

After spending about ten thousand dollars on clothes and fat gold chains, Inga and Lauryn suggested we stay at a hotel in New Jersey and go home in the morning. The two girls went swimming in the pool inside of the plush hotel while Nasir and I talked.

"Check this out, Nasir," I began to explain. "Me and my boys ran into a little bit of luck and I want to help you and your crew out like I promised. Do you have any boys that could move coke?" I questioned.

"Fuckin' real," Nasir answered. "I know mad niggas in Marcy, Queensbridge, and Parkhill that want to get money but can't get their hands on shit," he explained.

"Alright, look Nasir, I'm going to give you two bricks and you do what you have to do to get on. But when you finish you owe me twenty thousand dollars and you have to keep buying from me. Is it a deal?"

"Hell's yeah," he excitedly answered.

"One last thing, Nasir. Don't say anything to the girls about this shit, all right? Inga is a good girl so take care of her and do right by her and fuck all them other borough bitches, okay?"

"Thanks, Ant," he said. "I promise I won't screw you."

The girls arrived in the room from the pool.

"Y'all better not be talking about no bitches," Lauryn said.

"Stop acting jealous, girl, and let's go to bed."

The next morning we dropped off Inga and Nasir at home and headed back to Philly. On the way home a lot of thoughts were traveling through my head, but the most important issue that stuck in my mind was Nasir. For some odd reason I looked upon him as the little brother I never had, and never did want anything to happen to him. That is why I chose to help him out. While driving on the turnpike, I glanced at Lauryn and noticed she had fallen asleep holding my hand. My baby was happy and so was I. As I looked at her face it seemed to have a glow and she appeared to have gained a few pounds, maybe it was my imagination.

The next day as I was walking to the corner store to pick up a newspaper, Sam yelled from across the street to tell me to come over.

"I see you bought a new car, a lot of jewelry and some fancy clothes," he stated. "You know what, Ant," he continued. "You remind me of myself when I was your age," he declared.

"Sam, that's quite a compliment coming from an old-timer like you," I replied.

"No son, that's a warning. Didn't I tell you before not to go buying all that fancy shit because it's only going to draw the man to you?"

"Yeah, Sam," I explained, "but damn, can't I look good?"

"Alright, don't listen to me, little brother," he emphasized. "A hard head makes a soft ass," he mumbled as he walked away.

The Family

"Fuck him," is what I thought to myself. He probably was upset because I dressed better than he did and I drove a better car.

Within a month we made over five hundred thousand dollars to purchase again. So we contacted Mr. Cruz and followed the same routing meeting Cheryl and Sandy in New Jersey. Nasir came to Philly with another one of his homeboys named NORE to pick up what I had promised him. I sent big Tone with the two key loads to meet him at the Amtrak station on 30th Street.

While getting a hair cut at the Philadelphia Hair Company, the most frequented barbershop amongst high rollers, Lauryn paged me leaving nine-one-one as a code. I called immediately, then headed across town to see what the problem was.

"Anthony, I'm pregnant," she cried as I walked on the porch. "What do you want me to do?" she asked.

"I want you to have the baby," I answered.

"But Ant, you know I cannot stay in my parents' house with a baby," she explained.

"Don't worry about it, baby. I planned for us to buy a house in Wynnefield," I assured her.

"I love you, Anthony."

I told the boys that Lauryn was pregnant and the first issue that came up was who the Godfather was going to be. We already designated Nasir and Inga to be the Godparents, so that would end the confusion.

Meanwhile, Maurice told Shawn and Dante that he was having problems with a rival dealer named Jabril, who was robbing our houses and threatening our customers. We drove to West Philly, picked up Maurice, and then told him to point out the guy who was responsible for sticking up our houses. After riding around for an hour Maurice pointed to a short, stocky built guy standing on the corner in front of a deli.

"I'll handle him," Mark stated while exiting the car. "Excuse me, cuz, may I talk to you for a minute?"

"And who in the fuck are you?" the guy answered.

"Look, man, I don't want any more problems with you fucking with my business,"

The Family

Mark said while brandishing his nine millimeter.

"Alright, that's cool, brother," he said looking back as he walked away. "You got this one."

Mark hopped into the car, and we pulled off, leaving Maurice on the corner of Fifty-second Street.

By the time we reached South Philly, Maurice's mother called my house and left a message that he had gotten shot in the head, stomach, and chest. We went to the hospital to check the condition of Maurice and we were told he was currently undergoing surgery.

"An example needs to be made of this motherfucker," Mark yelled. "If we don't do anything everyone will play us for pussies and rob us every time they need money."

"Yeah, something has to be done, but not right away because they will know we had something to do with it, and in turn it will bring unnecessary heat on us."

"What do we do then?" Shawn questioned.

"I don't know right now, but I'll think of something."

The Family

I dropped the guys off at their houses and drove home. While parking the car an older gentleman carrying a bucket approached the vehicle and asked if could he wash the car to earn a few dollars.

"Go ahead, old man," I said.

"How much money are you paying me?" he questioned.

"I'll give you ten dollars," I replied.

"Ten dollars?" he asked in amazement. "Can I make this a permanent job?"

As he washed the car, he began lecturing about life.

"You seem like a very nice young man," he complimented. "The neighborhood has obnoxiously changed because of the drugs and the crime. If black folks learned to respect one another and be aware of our inborn capabilities, our social status would be greatly enhanced. Especially here in America," he lectured. "Everyone is running around valuing cars, jewelry and all the materialistic things in the world and forgetting to cherish the best fruit of the orchard, and that is life."

He continued to speak upon how living in the ghetto was the best thing to happen to him

71

because it prepared him to cope with the ills of society outside of it. To look at him, one would never believe he was as intelligent as he seemed when he spoke. While gathering his cleaning supplies, he paused and looked directly in my eyes.

"You know what, young man," he groaned, "I've watched you grow since you were yea big, and I know that you come from a well-respected family, who gave you the best education. Now selling them drugs, and living that fast life is like having credit cards," he explained. "It's a lot of fun until you receive the bill. Now, can I get paid, young fellow?" he questioned.

I paid the ten dollars owed to him, then asked his name before leaving.

"You can call me whatever you want, but don't call me late for dinner." He laughed, then walked away.

I never saw him again, but his wisdom regarding life remained with me forever.

CHAPTER 7

"The new Tommy fucking Gibbs," a voice shouted. "Yo Ant, it's me, Vinny, cupcakes. Remember me? South Philly? Come here, I want to talk to you for a minute."

It seemed a little strange to be spotted by him in the busy section of Center City during mid afternoon. Me and the boys were downtown shopping and picking up the diamond rings we ordered from this Jewish Jeweler who was located on the elite block of Jewelers' Row. Vinny lit up a cigarette, then began conversing about the days of us working together at the Italian Market years ago. I anticipated this conversation leading to an incongruous one.

You know what? It sure did.

"Ant, I'm gonna cut through the bullshit and let you know what's up," he said. "Word through the grapevine is you and your boys over there are moving some big shit all through the city, and I believe in all fairness that we should get a piece of the pie also. We don't touch that shit anymore," he explained.

"We left that to the spics and to you guys. I

The Family

am not going to go into detail about how they pay, but they do. And it's only right you boys do the same. You have to remember my people are the ones who own the shipping docks and let those banana-eating motherfuckers bring that junk here. Capish?" he emphasized while pressing his index finger and thumb.

"Are you finished?" I questioned.

"First of all, this is not the fucking 70s, Vinny, and we ain't paying you shit, capish? Vinny, I knew you most of my life, and I know you are no more than a spoiled, punk ass white boy who was handed everything from his father. Now, if you want to start a war, make a move. But remember one thing, if you want ass you are going to have to bring ass. And I am prepared to bring mine. Are you?"

He threw down his cigarette, stared me in the face, then walked away. I knew by the way he departed, it was not going to be the end right there. We were not paying anyone shit or taking anyone's shit. The chips would have to fall where they may.

The Family

"What the fuck did Vinny want?" Shawn questioned as I was walking towards them.

"Nothing," I replied. I didn't want to alert the guys as to what was said, simply because they were not as passive as I was, and they would undoubtedly strike first. I wanted to avoid as much unnecessary trouble as possible.

We continued shopping then picked up our rings. They were certified two-and-a-half-carat flawless round cut white diamonds valued at thirty-two thousand dollars apiece. The initials N.R.P. were ambidextrously engraved inside of the gem. These initials, N.R.P., which stood for Nubian Ruled Plutocracy, would later become one of the most recognized names associated with transgression in the city.

When I returned home, Nasir was on the corner shooting dice with some of the boys from down the street. He brought this wild girl named Kimmy J. from Brooklyn to transport the dope from here to New York on the Greyhound bus.

"This is my gangsta bitch," Nasir unwittingly uttered, making Kimmy angry.

The Family

"I ain't no bitch," she came back with. "If I am a bitch, call me 'miss bitch', okay?" the bold girl yelled.

Kimmy had braids, and this made her look exceptionally young but her large firm breasts would reveal she was of age to be screwed. Her tiny waist, plump ass, and curvy hips would entice any married man to consider cheating on his wife. I was no different.

"Kimmy, give me your phone number and maybe we could get together from time to time."

"From time to time?" she sarcastically queried. "Well where is your woman?"

"She's probably out with your man," I answered as she burst into laughter.

We talked a while longer before Nasir became impatient and rudely ended our conversation. After completing our transaction, the two departed from the bus terminal by way of cab. Before leaving, Kimmy and I exchanged phone numbers and planned a weekend rendezvous in Atlantic City.

"No dough, no show," she hollered, shaking her head and pointing her finger.

The Family

While entering a taxicab, I could only stare and smile in amazement. I had previously promised Lauryn to spend the weekend with her because she claimed the baby was giving her complications and yearned for my comfort. There was no way in hell I was overlooking my date with this sweet young girl to be with Lauryn who was probably making the complications story up anyway. Even though I loved Lauryn, because of my newfangled wealth, slowly I was falling out of love with her. Kimmy, like many other girls, now seemed to capture my foremost interest.

A meeting was held later in the evening to discuss possible revenge for Maurice getting shot.

"I suggest we go and kill that motherfucker Jabril," Mark voiced.

"Me, too," Shawn and Dante agreed.

"No way do we kill this asshole because of this petty shit," I replied. I suggest we let this incident ride, and if another such occurs, then we do something about it. I'm not ready to abandon all of this shit by doing life in prison because he wounded a motherfucker that I'm not even related to. That is plain stupid."

77

The Family

"Alright, fellows, make this one history," Mark groaned. "But the next incident will be his ass, and that's my word!"

After the meeting, I met Lauryn at her house. We spent the night at a luxurious hotel on City Avenue. While making love to her, I came upon the strangest occurrence. The entire time I was stoking her my mind was on Kimmy. The next morning I was abruptly awakened by a screaming voice in the room.

"Who the fuck is Kim, Ant?" she hollered.

She found the phone number in my pants while digging for money to pay for breakfast, she claimed.

"Aw, baby, that a girl who works for Nasir and asked me if I could help her locate an apartment here in the city. So I told her I would call her if I bumped into something, baby, that's all," I pleaded.

"You have become such a fucking liar, Ant," she softly whispered as tears began to fall. "All of my girlfriends say they occasionally see you driving other girls around."

"Them bitches are lying and only attempting to break us up," I intervened before allowing her to continue speaking. "The truth is, baby, I love you so much and would never allow anyone to come between us. Do you understand that?"

Holding her soft hands I lied.

"Yes, I understand," she replied, agreeing to give me a hug.

"I have a surprise for you next week, Lauryn. A very big surprise."

"Ant, please tell me what it is."

"Nope, not until next week." From the look on her face I noticed that she was relieved by what I had told her. Deep inside, I knew I was wrong, but as long as she was happy, so was I.

On Friday morning we made the usual trip to New Jersey to meet with Cheryl and Sandy. The girls bought a double load this time without warning, because Mr. Cruz flew to Colombia to visit family, and was not returning for two or three weeks. Since we were unaware of Mr. Cruz's sudden vacation until now, we brought only enough for one load. Instead of the girls returning to New York with the same dope, we ill advisedly accepted the material and promised to foot the bill on the next transaction. This proved to be an erroneous decision because, for a bizarre reason, while breaking down the two hundred bricks, we discovered half of them were below par grade.

Dante called Sandy and Cheryl to inform them of the surprise can of worms we picked up and for them to contact the Colombians immediately. Since we were no longer being fronted any dope because we were able to flat out pay for the goods, this probably was an ingenious ploy by them to keep us in arrears. As long as we owed them, we'd be compelled to purchase their material. A sense of urgency on their part could have come to be because their prices had significantly increased since the beginning of the nexus, and deemed a new connection would be sought.

Within two hours June phoned the girls and relayed the message from Mr. Cruz for us to keep the cocaine and he would clear up the problem when he returned to New York. He knew we would have to do so because if we didn't after the first week we would be depleted of our material, and set to lose an enormous amount of gravy.

The Family

We were supplying some guys from Norfolk, Richmond, Durham, Atlanta, and Boston, so we consigned the defective bricks to them, which increased their stock and secured our debt. One hundred bricks at fifteen thousand dollars apiece promised a million and a half for our cartel.

On Saturday, Kimmy and I reserved a luxurious suite at the Taj Mahal in Atlantic City for the remainder of the weekend. We spent the day shopping on the boardwalk and gambling in the casino. While we were in the Bally shop, Lauryn's mother paged me and informed me that her daughter was in labor and wanted me to get there as soon as possible. Kimmy was having such a good time that there was no way of telling her I was leaving, so I phoned my little sister and asked her to accompany Lauryn in the hospital. Also, I told her if Lauryn questioned as to where I was to inform her that I was in Florida awaiting the next flight.

By that evening Kimmy and I had spent nearly fifteen thousand dollars between shopping and gambling. While relaxing in a luxurious hotel room, Kimmy graced the floor in a rich satin jacquard robe, exquisitely finished with a satin charmeuse shawl collar and cuffs. Under the robe featured a gold Venice laced bra with a matching thong bikini. We made love all night. Her loving fell nothing short of what I expected. The feeling of her tight walls and the taste of her love kept me hard all night. The next morning we immediately started where we left off.

"Baby, are you enjoying yourself?" she softly whispered as she was licking my balls. "I'm thirsty, I want you to give me something to drink," she moaned.

Almost immediately after hearing that I ejaculated like never before, entirely in her mouth. All I could do afterwards was lay in the bed and twiddle my toes.

"I want to see you again," she stated.

"You will," I assured her. "I don't want you carrying shit for Nasir anymore, Kimmy," I demanded. "Before you leave I'm going to give you twenty thousand dollars for a new car and an apartment."

"Twenty thousand dollars?" she questioned in amazement.

The Family

"And what else do you want from me?" she joked while hugging me. Then she went down again.

It was checkout time and Kimmy's limo back to New York had arrived, but before leaving she thanked me for a wonderful weekend and looked forward to hearing from me soon.

I drove back to Philly to learn that I had a six pound, eight ounce beautiful baby girl born on Saturday night. Lauryn named her Shatora Amani Preston. Before reaching the hospital I bought some balloons and a card for her and the baby.

As soon as I entered the room, her mother rolled her eyes at me then walked out.

"Some bitch was more important to you than seeing your first child being born?" Lauryn sobbed after refusing to let me hold the baby.

"Lauryn, don't start," I begged. "Do not start making false accusations, this is not the place nor the time."

The baby was light-skinned like Lauryn, but had my eyes and nose.

The Family

Dante, Mark, and Shawn arrived at the hospital with more balloons and bad news. I was told Jabril and his boys robbed two of our four houses for over seventy-two thousand dollars and two kilos.

"If we would have handled this shit from the get-go, this would have never happened," Mark emphasized.

"While you were out of town boning that bitch, we were getting robbed," Shawn belted out.

"This is all my fault?" I responded. "What the fuck are y'all, the three stooges or something?"

Between Lauryn's arguing and those motherfuckers' attitudes, I had an enormous headache, so angrily left the hospital.

I went straight home and called Kimmy to tell her I needed to see her right away. I devised a plan on how we were going to handle this bullshit with Jabril and his boys, and it included Kimmy's help. Dante called Kobe and Eddie, two crips from Van Nuys whom he befriended in California, and flew them in town immediately. Everything was set up to take place at Cosmi's, an exquisite

The Family

Italian restaurant on the South Side, on Friday night.

We had an exceptionally busy week for some odd reason. We sold double of what we usually sell during the week. By Thursday, the million and a half we had consigned to the out-of-towners had been paid in full. We paid the Colombians their money and divided the remainder among the four of us. On Friday night, I sat at Cosmi's and waited for Kimmy and Jabril to enter the restaurant. The previous Wednesday, Kimmy drove to Philly and Jabril was pointed out. Her job was to get acquainted with him and lure him to the restaurant on Friday night. She did exactly that.

As she and Jabril entered the crowded room, she lead the way to a table in the back of the restaurant, which was strategically planned because it hindered the chances of Jabril successfully escaping. Ironically, Kimmy implemented that part of the hit. She seemed to enjoy being a part of this more than I did. I sat at an adjacent table with my back towards them, but was able to eavesdrop on their conversation.

85

The Family

"Jabril, you wear expensive clothes and have a very nice car," she convincingly complimented.

"It wasn't always like this, baby," the soon-to-be-dead-man replied. "I paid my dues."

"I know you have mad women," she voiced in her New York accent.

"Well, you know, a true player is hard to find but they're easy to recognize," he arrogantly quoted. "That is why I meet a lot of bitches."

I gave Kimmy the signal to let her know that now was the time to begin executing the plot. The conversation at their table suddenly changed as Kimmy's manipulative persona suddenly took effect.

"All of you niggas is stressing me the fuck out," she uttered out of the blue.

"Stressing you the fuck out?" he questioned. "Hell, I just met you, bitch."

"Bitch, is that what you called me, motherfucker?" she said.

As she continued speaking a waiter approached the table to inform her she had a courtesy call at the booth.

86

The Family

"Some days, you are going to be the pigeon, and, some days, you are going to be the statue, pussy," she sarcastically warned him as she walked away. He sat in a state of confusion and waited for her return. About two minutes passed and then Kobe and Eddie approached his table.

"Pardon me, dudes, these seats are taken," he informed them.

"We did not come here to talk, motherfucker," the gunmen could be heard saying, while drawing their automatic weapons.

Jabril was hit with over fifty rounds in the head, neck, and chest, and he died immediately. The crowded restaurant panicked and ran towards the exits. I blended in the crowd and managed to leave safely.

The four of us met at a hotel in Cherry Hill, New Jersey where the gunmen received their five thousand dollars pay, and where Kimmy and I spent the night.

"How did I do tonight, daddy?" she asked of her role.

87

The Family

"You did a good job, baby, and you know what comes along with doing a good job, right?"

"Yeah, I get paid," she jokingly replied, but serious. She received ten thousand dollars, not so much for what she had done but for the way she made me feel. I was more comfortable with her than I was with Lauryn.

The next morning, after crossing the Walt Whitman Bridge, I purchased a newspaper to see if the incident had received any media attention. It did, and the police had no suspects or motive. A perfect hit! We celebrated that evening by giving all of the workers the night off and hosting a lavish party at the Marriott, with ten Oriental and Swedish escorts from Manhattan. Lauryn was paging me all night, but I ignored her calls and continued partying. It felt good being on top and having all of my boys around me.

What more could a man ask for? We had all of the women, cars, and jewelry money could buy. We were bringing in so much loot that the ones and five-dollar bills that were grossed after each complete shipment were usually spent on women. No one ever realized

The Family

that in the mid-eighties and the early nineties, that car dealerships, clothing retailers, jewelry stores and bailbondsmen here in Philadelphia grossed the top revenues of every major city across the globe for nearly five years, all because of us. Even the police department was receiving a piece of the action. When they weren't earning money by going to court because of the increasing drug arrests, they were either on our payroll or were stealing from the boys. Later, investigation of the police department undoubtedly proved just that. We were the new brokers in the city of brotherly love. Our money was stacked so high, if we'd jumped off it we'd be committing suicide.

The Family

CHAPTER 8

"Brothers and sisters, do you love the Lord? I can't hear my flock. Brothers and sisters," he repeated, "do you love the Lord? Well, I do, too. And if loving the Lord is wrong, then I don't want to be right," the one-time pimp turned pastor shouted.

He was Reverend Larry Williamson who owned First Southern Baptist Church on Delaware Avenue. Reverend Williamson and Sam were inmates back in the seventies. The Reverend had told him the church was suffering financial woes, and soon the doors would close if ten thousand dollars was not raised to pay back taxes.

Sam asked me to subsidize the debts of the church, and advised that by doing so, it would be considered a benefit to the community. The timing couldn't have been better because Mr. Cruz relocated the warehouse from New York back to Florida. To get our material, a trip once a month was necessary.

After consulting with the boys I suggested sponsoring a free bus excursion to Disney World for the underprivileged kids of the city,

91

The Family

promoted by Reverend Williamson's church. This act of kindness would benefit the church children, who probably would have never seen Disney World otherwise, and, most importantly, it benefited us. We could convey at least five hundred kilos a month on three chartered buses without being bothered by the highway patrol because the church name was on the buses. And who ever bothered church buses on the expressway?

The others OK'd my suggestion, so I took twenty-five thousand dollars to the Reverend. Ten thousand dollars was for taxes, another ten thousand dollars was for him to get the buses up to par, and the last five thousand was for his pocket.

"The Lord will bless you, son," he responded, while almost taking my hands off grabbing the money.

"I am sure he will, Reverend. I am sure he will."

I took a week off to vacation in Puerto Rico with Lauryn and the baby. We had a wonderful time snorkeling, horseback riding, and swimming in the aqua green Caribbean Ocean. A private tour guide drove us to the cities of Arroyo, Bayamon, San Juan, and Ponce. Of all the places we visited, the city of Ponce was the most intriguing. Lauryn fell in love with all of the jewelry and clothing stores. I was impressed with the food and the hospitality of the natives. Everyone seemed so polite and carefree.

We were so impressed with Ponce, Lauryn suggested we purchase a villa since land is inexpensive down there. We made an agreement with a realtor to purchase two villas for a total of fifteen thousand dollars. I told her one villa was for us and the other was for the boys. Actually the other villa was for Kimmy, who had had a fit when I told her I was vacationing for seven days with Lauryn.

I called Mark in Philly to find out if everything was satisfactory, and as usual it wasn't. Someone had set fire to three of his cars and the landlord of his grandparents' home of forty years decided they were selling the buildings. Coincidentally, the landlord of his grandparents' home was Vinny's uncle, Joey Tellati.

Putting the two incidents together, Vinny was the likely culprit for the explosion of

Mark's automobiles. Also, Shawn had befriended a guy named Pakistani Mike, who was a big-time heroin dealer from Harlem who recently was doing business in Philly. Shawn knew better than dealing with anybody who was in the smack business.

We had previously vowed to never involve ourselves in heroin. Selling heroin would not only jeopardize his freedom, but would also grasp the immediate attention of the feds. This was a definite violation of the rules and should be addressed immediately.

After speaking with Mark I phoned Kimmy only to receive more bad news. Her period was late, and she thought she might be pregnant. She also told me if I was not home by tomorrow our relationship was over. I could not stand losing her, so I contrived an excuse so Lauryn, the baby and I could get a flight back to the city the next morning. She was furious, but I promised to stay a whole week with her next month in our newly acquired villa.

On the flight home, Lauryn and I engaged in a lengthy conversation, where she pleaded with me to get out of the fast life because of a dream she had in which I was killed. Usually, I paid little or no attention when she would ask me to do such. But this time, I actually considered it.

"What would I do about money?" I asked her.

"Get a good job," she replied.

"Lauryn, you like nice things, and so do I," I began to explain. "With working a regular nine-to-five you can't afford those types of luxuries."

"What is more important," she asked, "money or your family?"

I totally disregarded the question. Then I tried another scapegoat.

"What about my boys? I can't just leave them hanging, baby," I explained. "Look, in due time I am going to get out of this shit. I need you to hang in there a little longer, okay, baby?"

"You promise?" she whispered in my ear.

"Yeah, baby, I promise."

The next day after returning to Philly a meeting was called at my house. Everyone was present, except Shawn, who arrived two hours late. During the meeting we discussed the fire bombings of Mark's cars and, also, Shawn's involvement with Pakistani Mike. He was warned to stay away from him and then was told why. He responded by stating that he had the right to be with whomever he pleased, and whatever type businesses he participated in had nothing to do with us.

Many times we had disagreements, but never had anything such as this come about. After a little more forceful convincing he agreed to cease all ties with Mike and leave the heroin alone. For some reason I did not believe he was sincere with his truce. This shit would surface again.

I was absolutely correct. About two weeks later we were informed by a reliable source that Shawn had instituted a partnership with Pakistani Mike in distributing heroin in Philadelphia, Camden and Newark, New Jersey. The remaining three of us needed to meet to discuss what should be done, so we called another rendezvous.

"We are going to have to remove the weak link to tighten the chain," Dante expressed.

"What do you mean? Kill him?" Mark questioned.

"You're goddamn right," he answered. "Obviously he does not give a fuck about us, so why should we care about him?" Dante rationalized. "He didn't offer to cut is in on the deal. This motherfucker is plain greedy."

"As much as I despised Shawn's demeanors, I do not think we should kill him," I opined.

"It comes down to either him or us, my man," Mark stated. "Let's wait until after the first bus excursion to Florida to pick up the five hundred bricks because we need the money," he continued.

The mere thought of having to kill my partner made me realize that very moment that it would be the beginning of the end. If they felt that way about Shawn, the same rules would apply to me. My only rationalization concerning this matter was Shawn had brought this upon himself. There was nothing I could do about it.

For the next two weeks before we were leaving for Florida, we continued our relationship with him and acted as if we did not know anything. The big day came with us

97

chartering fifty underprivileged children from across the city, to Disney World.

Lauryn and the baby partook in the excursion as did Shawn, Dante, and Mark's family. Ironically, on the journey to Florida I was seated with Shawn's mother. She revealed to me several childhood pictures of him and his older sister. I felt very upset, because I was sitting next to a mother whose only son I was going to kill. Trying to block it out of my mind did not solve the anxiety. All I could visualized was the photograph of Shawn and his sister at the zoo.

We made it to Disney World and the Colombians met us in a nearby hotel with the dope, as the others remained in the amusement center. We remained in Orlando for two days, but I was unable to enjoy myself. The worry triggered my ulcers to act up severely, and I was rushed to a nearby hospital.

Upon arriving in Philly, the drivers of the buses were instructed to drop everyone else off at the church, then take the vehicles to a warehouse in Wynnefield. The four of us unloaded the five hundred kilos from the undercarriage of the bus, tipping the drivers five hundred dollars each.

While inspecting the shipment, I received a page from Lauryn who told me to immediately come home. As I pulled up in the driveway I spotted Kimmy's car parked across the street with her and her girlfriend hollering into the car phone. Kimmy did not see me enter the house.

"You better tell that crazy little New York bitch to get the fuck from the front of my house," Lauryn demanded. "She is on the phone hollering," she continued while handing me the phone.

Instead of speaking I hung up the receiver and tried to rectify the situation by going outside to speak with Kimmy.

"Get your shit and let's go," she insanely demanded.

"Kimmy, go to New York and I'll call and explain everything to you tomorrow," I pleaded.

She called me every name in the book, then spit in my face and pulled off. I returned to the house to find Lauryn packing the baby's belongings.

The Family

"When you get your shit together, call me," she stated. "As a matter of fact, don't bother calling. When you want to see your daughter, I'll bring her to your mother's house."

Before leaving, she placed all of the diamonds I bought her on the table and told me to give them to my little ghetto bitch. She also had gone for a doctor's checkup only to discover she was eight weeks pregnant.

Everything seemed to be going wrong. But instead of sobbing in my own sorrow, I went to an Oriental massage parlor for the rest of the night to relax.

I was so into myself that nobody else's feelings mattered. All I cared about was my money, and fuck everything else because I knew Kimmy could be bought back and Lauryn would eventually come back like always.

Midway through the week, the night of Shawn's departure from the world was planned. Mark carefully plotted the hit. Making me responsible for picking Shawn up in my car and driving to our clubhouse on Olney Avenue. We played spades and joked the whole night, reminiscing about the old days. Shawn seemed to be really enjoying himself, more so than I saw him in a long time.

My stomach was getting upset, and drinking E&J brandy was not making matters better. Throughout the night, Mark occasionally glanced in my direction to observe my behavior. I had no idea when or where they were going to whack him but I felt it was coming soon. It became painfully obvious that something was wrong with me being silent.

"Ant, forget about tonight," Mark slid over and whispered. Just at that moment I felt a sigh of relief, and the monkey that was on my back had been removed. Although Shawn had not complied with our orders prohibiting him from dealing heroin, he was still a close friend. I could not justify any situation that would be so severe whereas taking his life would be mandated.

We played spades until three o'clock in the morning, and then Dante suggested we ride to Harlem to shop at the Dapper Dan clothing store. While we were on the expressway

The Family

Shawn and I engaged in an intricate conversation.

"Ant, if the other guys plotted to kill me, would you go along with it?"

He asked almost as if he knew something was going down.

"Hell, no, I wouldn't go along with it," I deceitfully responded.

"My mother told me you and her were talking during the trip to Florida. and she thinks you are a very nice and intelligent person," he continued. We sat in the back seat of the Mercedes coupe and chatted a while longer.

Shortly after we passed Metuchen and Perth Amboy, Mark pulled over the car and said he was tired and felt he was no longer able to drive. Dante had fallen asleep and I was too exhausted to drive so Shawn took the wheel and Mark sat in the back of the car with me. I dozed off, hoping that when I woke up we would be in New York.

As I was sleeping I heard a sudden boom, almost like a cannon. I immediately woke up to see Shawn's brain splattered against the windshield. Dante grabbed the steering wheel, coasting the car to the guardrail. Mark had shot Shawn in the back of his head with a Russian-made glock forty-five semi-automatic.

I had to push Shawn's lifeless body forward, which was surrounded by a pool of blood, and climb out of the car. The three of us walked along the expressway to the nearest exit then caught a cab in Newark back to Philadelphia. My heart would not stop pounding because of how suddenly all this happened.

Dante and Mark told me all this was planned and they had no intentions of going to New York. Two days later, the New Jersey coroner's office contacted Shawn's mother and asked if she could come identify the body. She was too distraught to drive and asked if I would be so kind as to take her. I agreed, then drove to her home to pick her up. My hands were shaking so much before I reached her home I took four Xanax pills to relax.

"How could someone do this to my baby boy?" she cried, draping her arms around me.

The Family

I even started crying, then promised I would find the person responsible for this and have them taken care of.

When we reached the medical examiner's office, Shawn's face appeared on a screen so she could identify him. She fainted to the floor after seeing half of his face removed. I became nauseous and immediately ran to the bathroom. This was as bad as it could get. When I returned home I called Lauryn and asked if she would come back home. I promised to leave Kimmy alone, vowed in six months I was getting out of the game.

"Anthony, what happened to Shawn?" she questioned. "Please do not tell me you had anything to do with that," she begged.

"Tell me, Ant," she persisted.

After I didn't say anything she read between the lines and started to cry.

For the first time since we started this business I felt sorry for getting involved in the shit. I knew getting out of the business would be harder than getting in. Now that I was a part of two murders, there was no way of turning back. I was in need of a break so Lauryn asked her mother to watch the baby for a week, while me, her; Inga and Nasir flew to our villa in Ponce. Nasir told me he was getting out of the game in a few months because he made enough money to pay Inga's way through college and to pursue his career in music.

"Get out of this shit while you can," he advised. "Ant, there is no winning in this game. There are only three places this shit will take you: the grave, jail, or rehab."

Here was this skinny young boy giving me lessons about a game that I taught him how to play. He proposed starting a partnership in a record label and buying realty in the state of Delaware. I told him I would think about it and get with him later on that.

After telling him what happened to Shawn, the remainder of our days in Puerto Rico were spent quietly. It seemed as if he did not want to be bothered with me anymore. Unfortunately, my intuition was correct, because that was the last time I heard from Nasir.

Returning home, we still had unsolved business to settle with Vinny, so I phoned him and arranged a liaison. We amicably resolved

The Family

our differences with terms never being disclosed to date. Having the Italians in our corner made life easier, especially with the police, because most of the locals were either relatives or friends. One hand washes the other, and both wash the face.

CHAPTER 9

"Thirty-six telephone-equipped luxury cars, three mansions, two villas in the Caribbean Islands, and moving over four million dollars' worth of dope a month. Those niggers must be stopped," bellowed the angry federal agent. "Lieutenant, do whatever is necessary to put these assholes out of business and behind bars. I haven't seen this many coons working together since slavery," he emphasized while lighting a cigarette.

"Hey, boss, what is the most effective approach the department may employ to do so?" the assistant posed.

"The most conventional way of infiltrating blacks is by using other blacks," answered the racist agent. "It worked with the Black Panther Party, NAACP, and every other colored organization in the past. Why would these losers be any different? We have two African-American officers from the northern district that specializes in dealing with black underworld organizations in the metropolis. Assign the two agents to the dangerous task of bringing these cowboys to justice," the superior instructed.

"Will do, commander," the frail officer replied, gathering paperwork from his desk. "Will do."

Lauryn and I had an extravagant wedding with over five hundred invited guests and family members. The wedding was convoked earlier than we planned due to her pregnancy. Mark was the best man while Inga was the Maid of Honor in the wedding. The weather was beautiful and everyone enjoyed themselves.

The highlight of the evening was a quartet who sang "Always and Forever". The four young voices were a group of boys from Philly who I heard harmonizing on South Street and decided to pay them to sing at the reception. Inevitably, the young group would later become critically acclaimed.

Our honeymoon was spent in the Cayman Islands, then flying to the exotic Polynesian Island of Tonga. My priorities in life were being put in proper perspective. No longer was I hanging out all hours of the night and chasing women. I decided to leave Kimmy alone for the sake of not losing Lauryn, my new wife.

During the last conversation Kimmy and I had, she questioned me as to what she was lacking to make me as happy as Lauryn did. It was not an easy question to answer but after giving it some thought my response left her clueless as to what I meant. To make me happy I told her I needed Faith. She took my departure rather hard but it was imperative I place my wife and child well being ahead of her feelings.

Taking heed of the advice of Nasir about starting a business, I opened five automobile detailing shops across the city and three in Camden, Trenton, and Newark, New Jersey. The excursions to Florida were routinely carried out on a monthly basis, which limited time with Dante and Mark. We sold the two North Philly corners of Eighth and Butler Streets and Fifth and Indiana Avenues to Spel and Angelo for five hundred thousand dollars respectively. Even though each corner generated as much as one million dollars in sales per week, we eliminated the hassle of bagging up the large amounts of cocaine every month.   Selling out now eliminated the headache that came along with dealing with junkies. Besides, we were their wholesalers anyway. The more they made, the more we made.

A friend named Lenny, who was supposed to have been serving a fifteen-to-thirty year prison term for Interstate trafficking of heroin, had mysteriously come home after serving only six months of his sentence. I had known Lenny for a while, ever since we played in Catholic youth organization basketball.   I thought nothing of him introducing me to his cousins from out of town. Their names were Dajuan and Todd. Dajuan was his cousin on his mother's side, originally from Staten Island, now living in Connecticut. He was a clean-cut, well-dressed man in his late twenties. His style of dress, that included sweatshirts, jerseys, and two-tone wallabees, made him look younger than he was. Todd was a distant cousin from Wister, Massachusetts who also wore similar apparel. The short stocky man who looked as if he was in his early thirties appeared to be more street educated than Dajuan, but the two worked well together. Lenny informed me that they were mediocre dealers and wanted a better connection so they could prosper.

A second meeting was arranged in Valley Forge, inside of the swimming pool. Having a meeting inside a swimming pool would ensure that neither of the men was wearing wiretaps. Mark and Dante asked if it was necessary for them to be there, but I assured them everything would be fine because they were kinfolk of Lenny. The meeting lasted only fifteen minutes because we got a late start due to heavy traffic and I was in a rush to get home to Lauryn and the baby. The initial purchase was unusually small for a person to travel out of the state with, but since they were family of Lenny's, special allowances were made.

In due time our business relationship turned into a personal one. On many occasions, Todd, Dajuan, and I would shop up in Yonkers or attend Knicks and 76ers games. Strangely, Lenny would never travel with us out of state. I figured he was probably on parole and did not want to go through the hassle of notifying his P.O. every time he crossed state lines.

Our second baby was due in two months, and Lauryn wanted to purchase a bigger home. We looked at several houses in upstate Pennsylvania before deciding to move to Villanova. The forty-five acre Colonial style house had five bedrooms, three and a half baths, and a two-mile man-man lake with ducks. A two-ton vault was installed in a secret area on the premises, where I maintained cash and expensive jewels. As much as two million dollars in cold, hard cash was secured in the safe at all times.

We had a relatively small house-warming party because Lauryn was due any day and couldn't stay on her feet long. Several of her friends attended with me only inviting Mark and Dajuan. We received very nice gifts but the present from Dajuan struck my attention more than any other. His gift was an old-fashioned black telephone with a weird-looking device on the wire connecting the base to the receiver. He said it was nothing more than a decorative piece that was stylized during the 50s.

112

The Family

Moving to Villanova prohibited me from frequenting the city as much as I used to because of the time it took traveling back and forth. Once or twice a week I would attend to the necessities of my detailing stores which usually was not much to do. The shops were of no use to the community other than drug dealers who could afford spending a hundred dollars cleaning their vehicles. Most of the customers were dealers being supplied by us anyway, so the money was recycled. Stupidly, I believed that owning low profit businesses would justify my wealth if questioned by the IRS or the feds.

Many a night I would cruise across the city to observe the fruits of our labor. During those years, despite the increase in narcotic arrests, all major crimes plunged here in the city. For instance, strong-arm robberies and burglaries took a nosedive because everyone was making money. Most hustlers along the East Coast would verify their most profitable years in business as being 87, 88, and up into the early 90s. No one could pinpoint why, but it was our connection with the Colombians. Dante began venturing in Chicago, Detroit,

113

and Cleveland, exchanging cocaine for artillery from a set of crips and a militant gang who controlled the cities' underworld. Several trips to Chicago confirmed his theory about the black militia being the most ruthless motherfuckers he ever came across. Even though most were hardened criminals, whenever we visited they showed mad love towards us. All of our connections seemed to be vibing, even in Detroit. My perception of the motor city was that they were wannabe Chi-town players. But I was eminently surprised. Everyone in Detroit seemed to have nice cars and they were either entertainers, basketball players, or pimps. Next to Philly, Detroit ranked as my favorite city, for enjoyment purposes.

Lauryn finally dropped her load, having a healthy six-pound, seven ounce boy named Justin. We argued about not making him a junior, but it was her decision and I had to live with it. He was named Justin Yusuf. Even though I knew Dajuan only a short period of time, he was named Justin's Godfather. Since he was unable to make children, because of a motorcycle accident years ago, he said he was honored.

He rarely spoke of his family, or took me to meet any of his relatives because he said a distant relationship with them was healthier. Over the course of time, Todd and his purchases were drastically increasing. It confused me as to how they were able to maintain their business operations as sole proprietors and sojourn with me as much as they did. One Thursday evening, after taking Lauryn to her doctor's appointment, I stopped over at my mother's house to make sure everything was all right. There was an envelope on the table in the living room addressed to me from Kimmy:

> *I have been thinking about the disagreement that we had the last time we spoke. I came to the conclusion that it does not matter who was right or wrong. All I know is that something has come between us, which has been getting worse with time. I hate not hearing from you, Ant, and I*

The Family

> *want to do what is necessary to*
> *get our relationship going again.*
> *I am willing to sacrifice whatever*
> *is necessary to make the first step,*
> *but I need your help. I think it*
> *will make the both of us feel a lot*
> *better.*
>
> *love always,*
> *Kimmy*

I made good my word to Lauryn by not responding to Kimmy's requests, but somehow she found the letter, which led to her moving to her mother's house, following an argument.

"Many married men will tell you, it is not only coincidence that 'cupid' rhymes with 'stupid' after you get married," said Dajuan.

We spent the weekend at a ski resort with two of his female friends. They were from Spelman College in Atlanta, Georgia. Unlike other weekends I spent away from Lauryn, this time I really missed her. On the night before we left the resort, Dajuan and I played chess and spoke at length about our pasts. He told me of the many hurdles he had to overcome in order to achieve his present day status. I confided in him about our Colombian cocaine suppliers and all of the murders I partook in. He was an attentive listener, seeming to grasp every detail of every issue I shared with him. Despite the success I had been experiencing lately I was not sure of whether or not this was the lifestyle I really desired anymore.

"There is nothing worse than working hard for something you want, only to realize when you get it you're not sure if you really want it," Dajuan added.

Judging by his conversations, common sense would rule; he was either well educated, or he was not who he said he was. Not only was the brother street smart, he was legal savvy as well.

During the middle of our last chess game he received a page from Todd. He informed Dajuan about a mutual friend of theirs who had called offering an unbelievable deal. His name was Jamar from New Rochelle. He had supposedly counterfeited twenty million dollars of fake twenty, fifty, and hundred dollar bills, and was wholesaling them for close to nothing. Calling his bluff, I instructed him to call Jamar and arrange a meeting so I could inspect the bills.

Surprisingly, Jamar showed up at the New Brunswick hotel. He was a tall, light-skinned brother, sporting dreadlocks. Your first impression of him was that of a pretty boy trying to play Scarface. The bills were as crisp and authentic as the real ones I brought along to compare. For two and a half million dollars of real currency, I was told I would receive ten million dollars of counterfeit bills.

"I need three or four days to speak with my partner," I told him.

I would relay my decision via Dajuan and Todd. Dante was all for the deal after assuring him the bills would be able to be passed along. Mark was a different story because he was content with his lifestyle, and had no desire of changing it.

"If it ain't broke, don't fix it," he quoted. Mark enjoyed possessing ghetto glory so much he retained the two other corners of fifty-second and Market Street and Seventh and Snyder Avenue.

118

The Family

"After this deal, the three of us should retire from the game and live legitimate lives," I persuaded.

He refused the offer. Ever since we were kids, Mark always knew the art of making money but somehow found ways in which to inappropriately invest it. Never have I encountered a person so penny wise, yet so dollar foolish.

The Family

CHAPTER 10

"Baby, this is it, after this deal I am officially out of the business," I told Lauryn, before leaving to meet Jamar, Dajuan, and Todd at the Marriott near the airport.

The original meeting place was New Brunswick again, and, between Dante and I, we possessed five million dollars in cash. We sold all of the cocaine we had on the streets and canceled our contract with the Colombians. They were unhappy with our decision but wished us the best of luck.

I knew it was going to be a perfect chapter ending because of this deal. Todd asked if we could bring Mark along even though he declined the offer so he could meet him anyway.

Ironically the day before the deal was to take place, Mark had gotten strangely arrested for what neighbors witnessed to be a routine traffic stop, and had not been heard from since. I reckoned he was released and stayed over at one of his girlfriends' houses like he usually did. So I did not bother to think anything of it.

The Family

As we were driving across City Avenue in Montgomery County entering Philadelphia, a local police officer ran my tags, then pulled us over. Like always, he received an alias from Dante and me. He wrote the names on what appeared to be the paper for writing tickets, then slowly walked back to his car. After a few minutes passed by, he flicked his high beams on and off and allowed us to be dismissed.

Interstate 76 was jammed up, so we detoured to Interstate 95 and proceeded along. From the time we detoured off of the first expressway, a navy blue Ford Taurus had followed us until we exited near the hotel. The windows on the sedan were tinted so we were unable to determine who the driver was. As soon as we reached the entrance doors of the hotel, Todd and Dajuan emerged from their chairs in the lounge to meet us. He said Jamar was upstairs in the suite awaiting our presence.

The moment you opened the door the aroma of fresh money could easily be whiffed with little effort.

122

The Family

"You would be late for your own funeral,"
wisecracked the New Rochelle native.

"We ran into an enormous traffic jam on
the expressway and had to detour," I explained
to the dreadlocked man.

Dante remained outside of the hotel in the
car with our money, while we were in the
hotel counting the counterfeit currency. It
took us four hours to tally all the money but
the count was accurate. Two men he
introduced as Double E and Smitty from
Brentwood removed the money to another
room until our cash was counted. The
muscular built Long Island pair's only purpose
was to secure his money, Jamar assured me.
Since everything was correct on his part I
instructed Dajuan to give word to Dante to
convey our money upstairs.

At one period during the time we were
counting our money footsteps could be heard
outside of the hotel door, as if the elevator had
let out a considerable amount of people. A
sense of cynicism was endured about this deal,
since that occurrence. Occasionally Dante and
I would glance up, only to catch each other's

eyes looking regretful. Something did not seem right.

"Y'all short fifty-two hundred dollars," Jamar said while displaying his count on a piece of paper.

"Our money is correct, man. We counted it before we got here," Dante accentuated. "Let's count it again."

"Don't worry about the small change, maybe it was my mistake," he apologized. "Dajuan, go get the money."

As Dajuan stood up he pulled out a gun, as did Jamar and Todd. He ordered Dante and me to the ground and identified himself as a federal agent. The two other men who had been in the room with the counterfeit money burst in, along with ten other federal agents and US marshals. I lay on the floor in a state of shock, unable to comprehend what was happening.

As we were being escorted from the room, I turned to look at Dajuan. He put his head down and walked away. We were then transported to the federal building in Philadelphia, where we remained in custody.

The Family

On the day before we were to be arraigned I spoke to Lauryn and was told she was unable to contact Mark, and that no one had heard from him since he was arrested. I was removed from my cell and put in a secured room in the upstairs of the building.

That evening, in the middle of the night, a white federal agent entered the room and awakened me so that we could talk.

"Hi, how are you doing, Anthony?" he greeted as he glanced at the mug shot in his hand. "My name is Officer Mockerly, and I'm in charge of handling organized crime within federal jurisdiction here in Pennsylvania. I'm not here to play fucking games with you, scare you, or bullshit you.

"Here's the deal," he continued while revealing video and cassette tapes. "Every business transaction and telephone conversation you had in the past three years are here and here," referring to the two tapes.

"We have enough information to convince a judge that giving you the electric chair would be showing you leniency.

"Now Anthony, my man," he said, draping his arms around me. "You are young, have a beautiful wife, and two lovely children. Wouldn't you like to see them again, other than behind a glass window?

"I need your help in bringing down those Colombian pricks from Miami. And if you do so, I will personally see to it, that with good behavior, in five years, you will be on the streets again, fucking your mistress from New York. What do you say, brother? One hand washes the other and both, wash the face, remember?"

His knowing about Kimmy meant those assholes had done their homework. But I was neither impressed nor intimidated by the officer.

"Officer Mockerly, you fail to realize that you are not talking to a small-time corner boy. The Feds can't make deals," I explained to the frowning officer.

"Let me say it again, Officer Mockerly, the Feds can not make deals. Promises maybe, but not deals. So as for your deal, brother, read my lips: kiss my ass! Now, may I call my lawyer?"

THE FINAL CHAPTER

"All rise. This is the United States District Court, with the honorable Kevin Fitzgerald Buckwilder presiding in the criminal case of the United States of America versus Anthony Preston, also known as Anthony Butler, Tony Edwards, Antonio De Shawn, and Antoine King. Please remove all hats, close all newspapers, and remain silent while court is in session. Thank you!"

That was the court announcer making the entry speech for the judge whom was just entering the courtroom. Every alias that I had used during traffic stops or during routine searches had now surfaced in court. I had no idea that every incident that had occurred involving the police was being recorded and would be preserved for future reference.

The lead prosecutor was an asshole named Ronald King, who had acquired a reputation as being a hard-nosed district attorney that would go beyond the call of duty to have a defendant sentenced above the legal guidelines. Going into court, though, I felt reasonably comfortable because I had attained one of the city's finest criminal attorneys. His name was Vinchenzio Mirarchi, and he primarily dealt exclusively with racketeering cases. He was also known for being a vigorous lawyer whose claim to fame was gaining the acquittal of one of Philadelphia's most notorious mobsters named Frank "Little Frankie" Ianuzzi.

Mr. Mirarchi had instructed me, prior to going to court, not to show any sort of emotion or facial expression during the length of the trial. The reasoning behind this instruction was because if I did do so, it could subliminally persuade the jury to believe that the allegations made against me were indeed valid. He had also suggested that I have as many family and friends as possible to attend the trial in its entirety. That in turn could show that I had significant support from the community as well as from the home front.

I wore a one hundred percent virgin wool suit by Georgio Armani, a white shirt, and paisley printed tie, complementing the matching suspenders. Lauryn had bought me a pair of gators, but I had them sent back for a pair of black suede Cole Haans. The opening arguments began with the prosecutor reading my list of laundry charges. The list included murder, drugs, extortion, kidnapping, and corruption of minors.

As the prosecutor continued reading the charges, I had realized that something was definitely wrong with Mark's attorney not being present. Initially, our respective counsels had opted for separate trials and, surprisingly, the judge granted the motion. Even with the motion being granted it still would seem logical that his attorney be present at my trial, at least to take notes or to find out the outcome of the case.

The Philadelphia Times had referred to me as "the black John Gotti" in numerous articles that had been written pertaining to the trial. For the past two years, I had already crowned myself as the New York don anyway, so the comment made by the newspaper only served as a compliment. That was my mode of thinking at the time. As the district attorney concluded with the charges that were being assessed to me, the judge then asked me how I pleaded.

The Family

"Absolutely, one hundred percent not guilty, your honor," I sarcastically answered.

The courtroom erupted into laughter, as did I. My attorney emphatically instructed me to compose myself and to respond to the questions that were being asked of me appropriately. He also reminded me that I was on trial facing serious charges and that I could possibly become a prime candidate for the death penalty. I had never considered capital punishment as a possibility until Mr. Mirarchi had stated that it could become a likely suggestion from our opposition.

After my plea, Judge Buckwilder questioned the prosecutor as to what type of evidence was going to be manifested to support the state's allegations.

"Your honor," he stoutly retorted, "we have recorded numerous gang meetings, all implicating Mr. Preston as the ringleader of the N.R.P.s, commonly known as the 'Nubian Ruled Plutocracy'. To add to that, your honor, we also have a co-conspirator, now turned government informant, named Mark Diggs."

"What the fuck is going on?" I questioned Mr. Mirarchi. He briefly explained to me that

130

he had heard whispers of the possibility that Mark had been working along with the government to protect his own ass. The filled courtroom had also displayed a sigh of disbelief when Mark's name was mentioned. The prosecutor then cynically glanced at our table as to capture our reaction to his reply to the judge. I rested my head on the table and shook it in total shock. I recalled explaining to this fucking stool pigeon years ago that the feds cannot make deals because it is illegal, ultimately leaving the sentencing solely to the judge. At this point I knew that I was going to get fucked, by acquiring a lackadaisical attorney, who was either unknowing or unwilling to elucidate substantial facts pertaining to this probe. Oddly, after learning that there is a legal memorandum that is referred to as discovery in the judicial system, I was whole-heartedly convinced that Mr. Mirarchi knew of Mark's betrayal but had not informed me of that tiding. The judge had then called for a recess and for the court to resume in one hour.

During the break, as I was being escorted to the holding cell, Lauryn blew me a kiss and gestured thumbs up while my daughter could be heard crying, "daddy".

Once I reached the cell, I broke down into tears as a result of feeling ashamed to be in this fucked-up predicament in front of my mother, my wife, and my daughter. Now was not the time to be falling to pieces because it was imperative that I remain strong for my family as well as for myself. With so many bothersome thoughts emanating through my head, the recess had seemed to be perpetuated for about ten hours instead of one. Finally the court officers escorted me back to the media-filled courtroom, where a brief scuffle had broken out between two girls that I previously dated.

The judge called for the prosecutor to call the state's first witness to the stand. Mr. King had summoned Federal Bureau of Investigation agent George "Buddy" Wagner. The judge then ordered Mr. Wagner to raise his right hand, spell his last name, and to state his accreditation.

"Wagner, W-A-G-N-E-R, badge number 1776. I am a government agent assigned to handling organized crime factions in the tri-state area, which includes Pennsylvania, New Jersey, and Delaware."

"So you swear to tell the truth, the whole truth, and nothing but the truth on the words of the almighty God?" questioned the court officer.

"I do," he replied.

"Please be seated, Mr. Wagner," the judge instructed.

The prosecutor opened up by asking him if he saw anyone in court today that he could positively identify as knowingly violating the laws that were set by the forefathers of this country.

"Yes, I do," he answered, then he looked and pointed towards me.

"Okay, then, Mr. Wagner, can you please explain to the ladies and gentlemen of the jury, what exactly your investigation of this menace to society found?"

"Objection, your honor," Mr. Mirarchi intervened with. "My client's name is Preston and he should be referred to as such."

"Sustained," said the judge.

The Family

The prosecutor then continued with the instruction of telling the agent to explain the results of the Bureau's investigation.

"On November the seventeenth in the year nineteen eighty-seven, my superior officer, Commander George Mockerly, had received a phone call from a street informant, named Lenny, stating that a new black militant drug gang had been formed by the of the N.R.P.s, which stood for Nubian Ruled Plutocracy."

"Objection, your honor," my attorney had once again intervened. "Associating my client with any form of ethnic militia coterie is a superficial allegation that is no more than vicious hear say at best."

"Sustained," the judge uttered, gesturing towards the agent as to tell him to continue with what he was saying.

"Upon receiving this information from Lenny," agent Wagner recalled, "Commander Mockerly had immediately notified his superiors of this data. After several days of confidential investigation by the Bureau, the Commander later informed me that I was going to be the assigned dignitary to this onsetting probe.

The Family

"Upon being told of the ordinance, I then appointed agents Dajuan Coles, badge number one eight seven zero, and agent Todd Woods, badge number two one one zero, as undercover agents posing as drug dealers.

"A thorough investigation continued with agent Coles and agent Woods purchasing over three hundred pounds of powdered cocaine from Mr. Preston, as well as from his associates, over a thirty-eight month period. During the peak of this investigation, the department had been informed that Mr. Preston, along with two of the other co-defendants in this case, had become a prime suspect in three other unsolved murder cases occurring here in Pennsylvania and also in the state of California. Upon notification, homicide units along with the organized crime task force were made aware of our department's findings. After allied forces were merged together, with the direction of the Bureau, the probe was formally named 'operation shutdown'.

"Listening devices such as telephone bugs, wired buildings, and street informants all served as complementary aids in assisting us in completing our investigation.

"During this probe we had also learned that the N.R.P.s had links with Crips of South Central Los Angeles, a billion dollar Colombian drug cartel based in Miami, Florida, and an unnamed militant drug gang that tyrannized the metropolitan Chicago area. Again, further investigation did in fact prove that these cliques did share common bonds, ultimately resulting in the arrest of Mr. Preston and seven of his associates."

The agent finished giving his testimony and began exiting the witness stand as the judge had instructed him. Judge Buckwilder recessed the court for thirty minutes, after which examination was set to begin. While being escorted to the holding cell, I was overwhelmed by learning the fact that the only way the Feds know how much dope you have peddled over a specific period of time is because you sold the shit directly to them.

While I was waiting in the holding cell during the recess, Mr. Mirarchi had stepped through the door of the Iron Gate that separated the cells from the corridor area leading back to the courtroom. As he approached the metal bench on which I had been sitting, the despondent guise on his face made it obvious that something had gone wrong.

"Anthony, the prosecutor is offering us a plea bargain in exchange for a guilty plea from you," he dejectedly said. "If you plead guilty to all charges now, they will recommend a life sentence with the possibility of parole after thirty years, to the judge."

"As opposed to what?" I emphatically questioned.

"As opposed to being sentenced to die," he answered.

At that point the room seemed to become suddenly dark and my body became numb. Mr. Mirarchi had thought entertaining the possibility of the plea bargain would be in my best interest, because if I had to spend the rest of my life behind bars, it would be better than dying in the electric chair. But who the fuck wants to live under those circumstances?

I told him that I would need a little time to think about a decision because it was not an issue that could be immediately responded to.

The Family

It was approximately fifteen minutes before court was due to resume when I informed him of my decision to proceed with the trial and to fuck the prosecutor's plea bargain. If I was going down, I was not going down without a fight. Besides, I had paid Mr. Mirarchi well over fifty thousand dollars for his counsel.

Cross-examination began with Mr. Mirarchi asking agent Wagner if he or any of his affiliates, at any time, ever found me directly in possession of any kind of controlled substance?

"No," he responded.

"Well then, Mr. Wagner, at any time did you find my client in possession of firearms?"

"No, sir," he once again responded.

"Did you find any assortment of firearms or controlled substances on the properties belonging to my client, Mr. Preston?"

"No, sir, but the illegal drugs and guns that were seized during the raids of Mr. Preston's known safe houses did in fact belong to your client."

"Sir, that is not the question I asked of you," a smirking Mr. Mirarchi responded with. "Do you need me to reiterate the

138

question for better understanding, Mr. Wagner?"

"No, that will not be necessary," the agent scornfully replied.

"In granting the notion that your answers have been recorded with the responses of No, I now question you as to how in God's name you can lawfully associate Mr. Preston with these hideous transgressions?"

"Objection, your honor," the prosecutor said as he jumped out of his chair. "The defense is attempting to question the legalities of this case with an officer whose obligation is only to enforce the laws which were set forth by the founding fathers of this country."

"Sustained," yelled the magistrate. Shortly after Mr. Mirarchi completed the interrogation, the judge then ordered a fifteen-minute recess before bringing in the state's next witness. During this recess - since it was only a short break - I remained seated in the courtroom. I was unaware of who the state's following witness was, but I had noticed that additional sheriffs were making their way into the courtroom. Mr. Mirarchi had thereafter alerted me to the fact that the next

139

corroborator that was about to provide testimony against me was the state's strongest witness.

The court had now resumed as the informant was commanded to make his way to the now enclosed witness stand that had been shielded by what appeared to be three pieces of tinted plexiglass for the purpose of protection and to safeguard the identity of the stool pigeon. The prosecutor then told him to spell his first and last name for the court's records without revealing any more personal information unless being instructed to do so exclusively by the judge.

"Mark Diggs. That is D-I-G-G-S."

"Do you solemnly swear to tell the truth, the whole truth, and nothing less than the truth in this case on the almighty words of God?" questioned the court officer.

"I do," Mark responded.

Upon listening to my lifetime best friend begin to sell his soul to the devil, my heart had dropped to my stomach, and I felt slight drips of urine trickling alongside my leg. I would have never believed in a million years that this motherfucker, of all people, would do this shit to me. My anxiety had increased because I knew that if there was anyone that could have certainly validated the government's claim, it could only have been him, due to the fact that Shawn was dead and Dante had remained in custody.

As he began to testify against me, I could not stop thinking about the days when Mark and I would find ourselves in a villa in the West Indies, or just cruising down the lively streets of Manhattan snorting a sixteenth, simply politicking about life and how we had turned a small-time drug business into a lucrative organization. I could recollect a conversation that we had when we were in New Orleans at the Mardi Gras years ago. Mark had pointed out the fact that we were not born with silver spoons in our mouths but we had the obligation to our children to secure a luxurious lifestyle for them. He had also stated that because we had the Colombians backing us with all of the cocaine we needed, the Italians being in alliance with us, and having a Crip connection handling the dirty work, meant that we were a rare group of organized blacks. We had total control, which

141

in turn would put us under immediate scrutiny from the government.

Mark had always been the eyes that were in back of me, but now he had made a deal with the devil by aiding them in attempting to have me dwell in the belly of the beast for the rest of my life. He continued on with his deposition by detailing how we would spend several nights at exclusive hotels counting our illegal drug profits, at times reaching as high as two million dollars, in denominations of ones, fives, and tens. He also explained to the jury that after counting all of the blood money we would take trips to the casinos in Atlantic City to launder the money by going to blackjack tables. Exchanging dirty money for playing chips, then redeeming the chips at the cashier's booth for crisp fifty and one hundred dollar bills after only playing two hands. Lastly, he described in detail every murder contract that was ordered by us, including the homicide of Jabril, only placing himself as a lookout.

Mr. Mirarchi told me that Mark's testimony was the most damaging allegations that he had ever encountered in his twenty-five years of practice. Mark ended his testimony by labeling me as the mastermind that was responsible for flooding the streets of Philadelphia with cocaine and blood.

The mid-afternoon approached with the judge adjourning the court until the next day. Before leaving the courtroom, my attempt to kiss my mother was almost immediately obstructed by three emerging sheriffs that were called into the room prior to my exiting.

The next day Mark was called back to the witness stand to face cross-examination from my attorney. He attempted to detect any contradictions in Mark's allegations, but with the prosecutor objecting to many of Mr. Mirarchi's questions to Mark, it was virtually impossible to do so. The cross-examination was boring, non-effective, and brief, leaving some spectators yawning.

The plea bargain that was at one time obtainable from the prosecution was no longer available and I began feeling a sense of desperation coming from my defense counsel. The last testimony would come from the undercover agent Todd Woods. He had affirmed that he and fellow agent Dajuan

The Family

Coles had purchased about one hundred and eighty- one kilos of cocaine, with a street value of three and a half million dollars, over a three year period.

Ironically, it was later learned that agent Coles was not present at the trial because he was placed in a rehabilitation center by the department for the very same narcotic that he had worked so hard to get banished from the streets. Closing arguments began with the prosecutor summarizing the same information that was explicated by all three of the witnesses, and by my attorney attempting to simply exonerate me from any accused wrongdoing. The judge then charged the case to the jury to begin deliberations. The media and the spectators had remained until four o'clock in the afternoon when the judge decided to conclude deliberations for the day and to resume tomorrow.

That night I came down with a severe case of diarrhea, presumably from all of the worrying that I had suffered through the course of the trial. The next morning, the judge questioned the jury's foreman if a verdict had been reached. The foreman informed the judge that a verdict had been reached, handing a letter to the court officer, who then handed it to the judge. Silence filled the normally riotous courtroom as the standing foreman read the verdict.

"We, the jury, in the case of the United States versus Anthony Preston, find the defendant accused of murder and racketeering crimes, guilty as charged."

Loud sobbing from Lauryn and my mother could be heard throughout the courtroom. Afterwards, the judge instructed Mr. Mirarchi that sentencing was going to be held promptly at eleven o'clock tomorrow morning. The sheriffs then escorted me quickly out of the courtroom.

Mr. Mirarchi made his way back to the holding area and had apologized to me for losing the case, but made me aware of the fact that he had done everything that was legally possible in attempting to gain me an acquittal.

Before leaving, he also said that if I had any intentions of retaining him as an attorney to petition an appeal that he would need the money up front before starting the process. At that point I felt as though the whole world had

145

deserted me because of my fallen celebrity status. No more did I feel like "the black John Gotti", only like another dumb, drug-dealing nigger, chasing a bullshitting dream.

Sentencing day arrived with the judge asking if there was anything I would like to say to the court before he delivered his sentence. I stood up and began reading from a letter that Mr. Mirarchi had composed for me the night before because I was too nerve-wracked to write one myself. Imagine that, a decision between life and death is about to be levied upon me and I did not have the impudence or the sense to be able to compose an oration that could possibly safeguard my own existence from demise. As I had begun reading the apologetic letter I noticed that the judge was gazing at me with a glare of bewilderment, as to wonder if I was the person who was actually responsible for writing this letter. After reading my speech, he instructed me to remain standing as he prepared to formally announce his sentence.

"Mr. Preston," he said as he was taking off his glasses. "You have blatantly violated judicial laws, family values, and moral consciousness, with your inexcusable, asinine behavior. Amongst the law-abiding citizens here in Philadelphia, and to my own spectacle, you display little or no remorse for your demeanors.

"Judging by the facts that were substantial in the jury rendering a guilty verdict, I have no other choice but to sentence you to die for the hideous crimes that you have committed. Also, Mr. Preston, I sincerely hope that you find an inner peace within yourself, as well as in a higher power, before the time of your judging hour."

When I heard him sentence me to die, an empty feeling filled my body. As I was being shackled and led out of the courtroom, my mother fell to the floor crying as she pleaded to the leaving judge not to kill her only son. Tears had begun falling down my face and I began feeling lightheaded because of all the cameras and the lights in the courtroom. The next day I was going to be moved to a super maximum security prison that was located in Texas to begin my sentence on death row. While being shipped to my destiny of death,

The Family

many a thoughts was trekking through my head.

The mere thought of losing my freedom for ghetto glory and the sake of a fucking dollar just did not seem worth it at this point. During the process of me ruining my own black people, by making crack readily available to them, like most fruitless drug dealers in the hood, I had always attempted to fault the white man for my own misconduct. But the white man did not conspire with me to purchase the automatic weapons that paralyzed the little boy who was caught in the middle of crossfire, resulting from a drug war. He also did not have anything to do with me filling up the plastic vials with a substance that destroyed my neighbors' beautiful daughter which made her a prostitute to support her addiction for crack and my addiction to get a pair of Gucci's.

Towards the end of my fallen celebrity status, where were these so-called friends that I had referred to as part of my posse when I needed a character witness? Not one of these motherfuckers showed up during the trial to testify on my behalf. "The black John Gotti."

The Family

 How could that be when he received life and
I got death?
Maybe justice ain't color-blind.

THE AFTERWORD

My sincere gratitude to those who have journeyed with me in voyaging into the literary orb. I hope that you experienced as much enjoyment in reading my tome as I did in composing. Many shall wonder as to what motivated me in writing about such a topic. My foremost objective was to reveal the grim realities of life as a drug dealer. The fancy cars, expensive jewelry, and fast money are an insignificant compensation for the grief and sadness that accompany such a lifestyle. As a writer, I have the power to make people laugh, cry, hate, love, and think. So I strive to grasp my readers with education by way of entertainment. Many close friends have been murdered or incarcerated because of this plague. I watched my own life become severely affected because of an addiction to narcotics and its likes. Fortunately, with the help of God, self-determination, and my Uncle Kevin, I have learned to apply myself in a positive manner, which is manifested through my writing. So until we next share the expression of friendship, I now sign off.

Antonne M. Jones.

Antonne M. Jones
BIOGRAPHICAL INFORMATION
Date of Birth: April 23, 1972
Home Town: Philadelphia, PA

PUBLISHING CREDITS
Writer for Philadelphia Daily News
"Au pair Reversal Decried", November 22,
1997

"Suspect Descriptions Too Sketchy"

"Apology for Slur Won't Suffice; Abraham
Should Resign", June 25, 1997

"The Cocaine Crisis is Really a Matter of
Choice"

"Heading Towards Harmony", May 14,
1998

"Movie Madness", September 4, 1996

TITLES WRITTEN
"The Family: A Philadelphia Mob Story"
Eldon Publishing Co., June 24, 1999

ORDER FORM

Have your Discover, Visa, Master Card ready
On-line orders: www.eldon-pub.com
Postal Orders:
Eldon Publishing Company
PO Box 54742
Philadelphia, PA 19148

Please send the following book:

I understand that I may return any damaged book(s)
for a full refund - for any reason, no questions asked.

Name:_____

Address:_____

City:_____

State:_____Zip:_____

Telephone(____)_____

Shipping:

$4.00 for the first book and $2.00 for each additional
book.

Payment:

____ Check ____Visa ____ Master Card

____ Discover

Card Number: _____

Name on Card: _____

Exp. Date: ____/_____

ORDER NOW

ORDER FORM

Have your Discover, Visa, Master Card ready
On-line orders: www.eldon-pub.com
Postal Orders:
Eldon Publishing Company
PO Box 54742
Philadelphia, PA 19148

Please send the following book:

I understand that I may return any damaged book(s)
for a full refund - for any reason, no questions asked.

Name:_____

Address:_____

City:_____

State:_____Zip:_____

Telephone(____)_____

Shipping:
$4.00 for the first book and $2.00 for each additional
book.

Payment:

____ Check ____Visa ____ Master Card

____ Discover

Card Number: _____

Name on Card: _____

Exp. Date: ____/_____

ORDER NOW